NORTHERN

A third collection of Northern Crime Writing

Edited by
Martin Edwards

First Published 1998 by Countyvise, 14 Appin Road, Birkenhead, Wirral, Merseyside L41 9HH.
British Library Cataloguing in Publication Data.

A catalogue record for this book is available from the British Library.

ISBN 1 901231 10 0

CONTENTS

INTRODUCTION

This is the third *Northern Blood* anthology to be compiled by members of the Northern Chapter of the Crime Writers Association. It differs from its predecessors, which blended stories with true crime, in that this time around all the contributions are fiction.

We hope that the collection shows once again the range and high calibre of Northern crime writing. There is a good deal of convincing recent evidence of the quality of the contributors. Since *Northern Blood 2* was published, Val McDermid has won the CWA Macallan Gold Dagger for her excellent and chilling novel *The Mermaids' Singing* and Reginald Hill has been awarded the CWA Macallan Diamond Dagger in recognition of his outstanding career in the genre. In addition, Reg picked up last year's Dagger for the best new short story: "On The Psychiatrist's Couch", which appeared in the national CWA anthology *Whydunit?*, published by Severn House. It is also gratifying that the BBC TV series "Dalziel and Pascoe", based on Reg's long running series about mid-Yorkshire's finest, has achieved such critical acclaim and popular success. Meanwhile, "Heartbeat", based on Peter N. Walker's "Constable" books (written under the name of Nicholas Rhea) has become something of a national institution on our screens - its appeal is so strong that it continues to flourish despite the departure of Nick Berry and Niamh Cusack. I am therefore especially pleased that this book includes one of the very few short stories that Peter has written, together with "The Thaw", which Reg tells me was his first published short crime story.

The Northern Chapter of the CWA has been thriving for over ten years. It is, I think, a particular sign of health that this volume includes stories by no fewer than nine writers whose work has not previously appeared in the Northern Blood series.

One particular aspect of the compilation of this book which will long stick in my mind is the speed with which it moved from conception to execution. Members of the Chapter decided to compile a third anthology at the beginning of July 1998 - and publication was scheduled for the following November! Collecting all the stories therefore proved to be a more than usually exciting experience; I am enormously grateful to the contributors for their tremendous co-operation, which often caused them to put other tasks aside in order to contribute fresh stories. Eileen Dewhurst in particular gave generously of her time to help with the proofs. I am also grateful for the considerable efforts of John Emmerson and his team at Countyvise and the Birkenhead Press for their enthusiasm and their hard work on the book.

MARTIN EDWARDS
Editor, *Northern Blood 3*

ROBERT ADAMS

Robert Adams worked as a prison officer in HMP Pentonville at the time of the escape of the spy George Blake from another London prison, and later was acting governor of a penal institution. He then became a social worker and latterly a university professor with more than 80 edited publications and 10 books to his name, several on crime and punishment. He has given up most of his academic commitments to concentrate on writing fiction.

Robert Adams

THE HULL EXECUTIVE

On Thursday 22nd February 1996, Mr Rennison Potter, holder of a very modest 1974 degree in English from Hull University, sat at the place he had specifically reserved - one of those tables between two pairs of seats – nearest to the window, facing the rear of the train, in coach C, Standard Class no smoking, on the 7.05 Hull Executive from Hull Paragon to London Kings Cross. He always booked through the same agency, by telephone from the office, and made the same stipulations – though he always got muddled at the point where the travel agent asked him whether he wanted rear or facing, and in his confusion said things like 'Whatever you like, yes please, facing the rear'. This, of course, prolonged the call, much to his irritation, part of which was directed at his own failure to take charge of situations. No doubt it raised his blood pressure as well. He had to watch this, having had several little do's, a couple of visits to his G.P. and recently a spell under observation in Hull Royal Infirmary. His wife Enid, at 45 was three years his junior, but was five centimetres taller than him and wasn't slow at saying he needed to become more assertive if he wanted to make a break for a partnership in the firm of Andrews and Wallace Insurance Brokers, before he was fifty. She had become even more confident recently, since going to that therapy person. She had done lots of exercises the mere thought of which made him shudder. She had taken stock of her life, apparently, clarified her values and what she wanted from relationships. In a rare moment of frankness, she had told him on Valentine's Day only two weeks ago that even if their 23-year-old childless marriage wasn't going anywhere, she would never leave him. She just did not believe anything short of death should cause married couples to separate.

Rennison couldn't even cope with Enid raising matters like this. And he absolutely hated the thought of talking to her about his job prospects or their relationship. He could only cope by reducing life's complexities and problems to matters of money. He dealt with uncertainties by calculating their financial risk. If only he had sufficient funds behind him – say, £50,000 to clear his mortgage and give him a little surplus in the bank – he knew he'd feel so much more confident at work. As it was, he knew that when his colleagues whispered about him – once, he had overheard the word 'wimp' – they were probably right.

Enid didn't help. 'No', she said, 'it isn't a question of money. It's the kind of person you are that counts. Or how you act, because you can become the person you act. Becoming a true executive is largely a matter of dressing and acting the part.'

Now, as he looked out of the window at the grey mist over the River Humber in the early morning, some words of Albert Camus, from his studies 30 years ago, came into his head. 'Within each winter exists the invisible summer.' Why is it, he thought, that whenever I think of Enid, I find it so hard to imagine where summer really is?

This morning, the train was not particularly busy, but seats with a table still tended to be at a premium. When the train stopped at Brough, more people got on, heading mainly for the tables. Being a retiring individual, he thought he had made a mistake. At Doncaster, he knew he had when a middle-aged woman carrying a shabby, bulging leather briefcase, so self-consciously smartly dressed he sensed something over the top about her, walked down the gangway peering at all the numbers above the seats as though looking for a particular one and sat directly opposite him at the table. But it was too late to move now. It would have required an amount of confidence to gather up his coat and bag from the luggage shelf above his head and leave for another part of the train. Anyway, what if there were no seats in any other carriages? And he didn't have the nerve to go and sit at another seat in this carriage. People would be staring and thinking all sorts.

No words passed between them. By the time they were approaching Grantham, he was very relieved at the thought that this was the last stop before Kings Cross. He had studiously avoided eye contact with her, they still hadn't spoken, nodded or even smiled, so all would be as he preferred it. As the train slowed, the announcement came over the loudspeaker: 'This is your senior conductor speaking – we are now approaching Grantham – this is the last stop before London Kings Cross – Grantham the next station stop – please make sure you have all your luggage with you before leaving the train.'

She stood up and gathered her things from the luggage shelf above her head. Then, as if it was an afterthought, at the very last moment, when she was already making her way down the gangway in the moving queue of travellers who were leaving, she quickly folded the copy of *The Times* she had been reading and using to rest on while she apparently made notes on sheets from a notepad to help her do the crossword, and offered it to him, still without a word. He nodded his thanks as she smiled at him and laid it on the table.

It was some minutes before Rennison plucked up courage to scan the newspaper she had left. Was anyone staring at him? Did any other passenger think something indecorous had happened between them? He took a quick glance around. Nobody seemed to be paying any attention to him. He picked up the paper. As he opened it up and set its pages together as neatly as he could – he hated untidiness in people or things – he looked around and was reassured to find that the noise of the paper apparently wasn't causing any disturbance. He glanced quickly at the headlines, turned a couple of pages over and then the thought struck him that he'd find the crossword and see how far she had got.

Rennison never got past the Letters page. Pinned neatly to one side of Letters to the Editor was a small sheet of very thin paper – one of the sheets, no doubt, on which the woman had been scribbling. This is what he read:

'I have had my eye on you for some time. If you follow my instructions precisely, my husband will die through natural causes, and you will receive £100,000. At no time will you attempt to contact me. If you agree to take this on, when the train arrives at Kings Cross walk off the platform keeping to the left hand side. If you do not want to take it on, walk off at the right hand side of the platform. Take this paper to the toilet, tear it into small pieces and flush it away.'

To say Rennison was in a panic would be an understatement. Had he misread? A hundred thousand pounds. It was an absolute fortune, enough to set him up for life. He spent the next hour and twenty minutes going through all possible scenarios, ranging from pulling the emergency lever or asking the conductor to call the police, through to hiding in a luggage trolley, waiting till night time and creeping from the station and into hiding, or destroying the message and pretending the incident had never happened. He decided, and changed his mind, a hundred times over the rest of that journey. By the time the train reached Kings Cross, he was so confused he simply didn't know what he would do when he disembarked.

The Hull Executive pulled into Kings Cross a few minutes late, at 9.48. Rennison Potter took the decision of a lifetime. 'It's a Leap Year,' he said to himself. 'I *will* do it.' His legs were shaking as he stepped out of Coach C, crossed to the left hand side of the platform and walked slowly towards the ticket barrier. Nothing happened though. Despite peering this way and that, he could neither see the woman who'd got off at Grantham nor anyone else acting suspiciously.

By the afternoon tea break, Rennison was relieved that nothing untoward had happened during the day. He was pursuing some particularly complex actuarial statements for a local solicitor acting on behalf of a large company in the North East. That helped to push the incidents of the outward journey to the back of his mind. He returned to Kings Cross for the return journey to Hull that evening, as always, on the only straight through train, at 17.20.

He always followed a similar routine on his London trips. He went to the buffet and bought one of those large plastic beakers of tea and a baguette filled with the soft French cheeses Enid abhorred, made his way right to the front of the train, past the smokers in coach B and settled at an empty table in coach A. This was the way to avoid the noise and bustle of the middle coaches around the buffet. It was always crowded until Peterborough and Newark had passed, but by the time they had stopped at Doncaster the train was always nearly empty. He liked to eat his baguette, sip the tea, then have a nap till Peterborough, at which point the worst of the crowds of commuters would leave the train. Today was typical in all these respects, with one tiny detail which he noticed on waking up after his three companions had got out at Peterborough. Somebody, possibly one of them, had left a copy of *The Times* right under his nose on the table. Rennison glanced around him quickly. Only three passengers in sight and these all seemingly asleep. What should he do? He could pretend there had been a simple mistake and shove the paper unread into the nearest waste bin. Or he could move seats. When the train was three quarters empty, this was much more straightforward than it had been on the outward journey. He thought both of these were good ideas. Then he reflected on that first sentence in this morning's message, which he'd now destroyed, unfortunately, but which went something like 'I've been watching you for a good while.' No, it was 'had my eye on you', because he remembered asking himself rather skittishly, 'Where was the other one then?' So whoever it was could have left him a message this evening which identified, and therefore incriminated, him in some way. He would have to go through the paper and at least satisfy himself of that, before throwing it away and consigning this unhappy business to history.

He found the message, with the photograph of a man, pinned to the Letters page, exactly as before:

'At 19.30 Thursday 29th February, this man will take a sauna at the leisure and beauty suite on Barraclough Street in Hull city centre. He is a psychologist, has a weak heart and knows what precautions to take, including carrying medication to treat him should his heart go into a spasm, which he leaves with his clothes in his locker. This is number 30. He hires this number on a monthly basis. You will follow the instructions below to ensure that his locker key will not open number 30 so that when he receives the massive shock in the sauna, nature will take its course.'

All went smoothly, up to the point when Rennison fumbled the wax he was meant to be inserting in the keyhole of the locker and its owner came up quietly behind him: 'Having problems with my locker?'

The situation was bizarre. Rennison had been so shocked he'd had a dizzy spell and the man had to help him to the nearest bench so he could recover. In his confusion, he blurted out the essentials of the story and, to his surprise, the man didn't react.

'Dammit', said Rennison, 'I'm meant to be frightening you to death and I don't even know your name.'

'Peter, Peter Sugden. Dr Peter Sugden.'

'Peter, Christ!' Rennison blurted out, in a rare moment of verbosity, probably as a release for the severe stress he was experiencing. 'I'm causing a man called Peter to die. I don't believe this. Such an ordinary name. A psychologist for Christ's sake. You don't even look old enough to be retired. You've probably got patients to see, possibly even one or two are dependent on your particular knowledge of their condition, to keep them alive.'

Sugden laughed.

'A little off beam, old chap. I'm a psychologist actually. It's things non-medical which are my business, but, yes, I do have scores of patients, in my statutory work as well as in private practice as a psychotherapist, and some of them would doubtless miss me were I to disappear. I'm certainly not retired. To say nothing of relatives and friends of course. They'd be devastated. Not least because – with apologies to disappoint my dear wife – I'm A1 fit, no blood pressure, hypertension, heart pills, nothing.'

Rennison was baffled and his expression reflected this. Sugden suddenly shook his head with its mane of greying hair, as though ejecting some source of irritation from it.

'Now then,' he said, 'let me be straight with you. My wife has not hired you. At least, she thinks she has. But I knew about it all along. You see, she has some of the makings of a killer, but, thankfully for me, not all of them. I've been waiting for you to pop up – I wasn't quite sure where, but if you know someone is likely to appear, you're halfway there, aren't you? You probably haven't experienced it, but take it from me. So, she's been making these notes and leaving them in her diary at home and in one or two of her other private places and I've been intercepting and reading them. And now, you're the living proof of what she has planned.'

Rennison was the picture of total confusion and embarrassment.

'What can I say? I'm so terribly sorry for any upset I've caused. Whatever you want me to do –'

Sugden was becoming more genial by the second.

'My dear chap, please don't agitate yourself. We'll come to what might be done in a moment. But for now, accept my assurance that *you* haven't done anything which could possibly have offended me. The causes of offence lie entirely in my domestic arrangements. I'm afraid there is no way of an outsider understanding the hurt I've had to endure over the past five years or so.'

'What! You mean this has happened before?'

'Good grief yes. You're the sixth, or is it the seventh, person she's hired. But I have to tell you, at each stage, she's got worse. We have no children, you see. It was her ovaries, if you'll pardon the physical detail. But she never could accept it. All those years, the bitterness grew, and the anger, directed against me rather than at herself.'

'How terrible!'

'It is, but I can't describe what it's like to live with a woman who, without any other person knowing, plots continually to kill you.'

'Ghastly. It must be a nightmare.'

'But becoming daily worse. I'm unfortunately unable to specify any mental illness, or, with my contacts as you might imagine, I'd have had her sectioned before now and put into secure custody. However, there is another option, given that the deterioration is so rapid. You know, I expect, what I'm referring to.'

'I hope not.'

'Good God man, I'm not suggesting a cold-blooded murder. But she is a terminal case. I know that, on the basis of my knowledge of human growth and development. It is only a matter of time before she becomes completely possessed by this monstrous paranoia which at present only secretly gnaws away at her. I feel most deep sympathy for her condition and that is why I propose to do nothing to slow down her decline. In fact, I want to ensure that this terminal stage passes as quickly and painlessly as possible.'

'Oh.'

'Do you understand me?'

'Unfortunately, I believe so.'

'You must think back to her vicious plan to dispatch me.'

'Yes, oh my God, what have I got into?'

'I am simply intending to put her beyond the awful implications of pursuing that murderous intent. Otherwise, she would finish up under lock and key for the remainder of her life.'

'I see. What's her name?'

Sugden laughed at this bizarre question. 'Flora, not that I can see the relevance. Now, here's what I suggest we do.'

'*We?*'

'My good fellow, I can't do everything alone. That's why I'm asking you.'

'Look Sugden, I don't care how humanitarian your motives are, you don't get me involved. Okay?'

Sugden narrowed his eyes again.

'I'm sorry to say, but I believe you are already inextricably involved, Mr Potter.'

'And how is that?'

'Attempted murder? Conspiracy?'

At each of these words, Rennison physically shook. Sugden continued:

'And if anything happens, accessory before the fact, to unlawful killing? I would be loath to refer these to the police, of course, but you can understand the position from my point of view. I have to sort this out, in order to preserve life.'

'Your life perhaps, but not hers, as I see it.'

'Mine primarily, but the quality of life isn't there for her, and isn't going to be. So there is only one humane option, for both of us. Added to which, you haven't much choice. If you back down, I'll report you and the police will arrest you for attempted murder. Alternatively, as reparation, you can do this little job with me. Either way, you have some work to do.'

Rennison felt the room spinning.

'I'm feeling sick.'

'It's a funny thing about Leap Year,' said Sugden. 'There should be more institutions like the extra day in February when the woman can propose to the man. They should provide the chance for other sorts of communication to open up between people. I am a great believer in applying what mathematicians call catastrophe theory to families where interpersonal communication is lacking' said Sugden. 'Some people know so little about their own families, or their partners. Things plod along for years. But behind the scenes – or under the covers – the pressure for change is building up. Couples gradually change and grow apart. Suddenly, one morning one of them wakes up and – ping! – does something different and the other one says "what's happened to you?" But by then, it's too late.'

'Really,' said Rennison, who by now was sweating so profusely as to be feeling acutely uncomfortable.

Rennison swayed and nearly fell sideways off the end of the bench.

'I say, are you all right?' asked Sugden.

'Now you come to mention it,' said Rennison, 'I am feeling rather queasy.'

'If I were you, old man, I'd sit for a few moments. I say, are you always as pale as this?'

'Do I look ill? Oh my God, I can feel the pain coming on'

'You should have said. Being in such a hot, humid atmosphere is precisely the worst thing for a man in your condition.'

'I'm going to call an ambulance for you,' said Sugden. 'A man in your condition needs specialist help.'

'It is possible to know one person through another,' said Sugden.

'What do you mean?' Rennison panted.

'It's difficult for me to say this – confidentiality and all that – but as we speak I have such a strong sensation of having met you before. I realise it's through knowing Mrs Potter so well.'

Sometimes, a moment of realisation in a person's life occurs almost like a physical as well as an emotional shock. It hit Rennison suddenly that Sugden had been the person to whom she had been confiding, in her regular appointments over the past few months.

As he lay on the stretcher, waiting for the para-medics to wheel him into the ambulance, Rennison saw Enid approaching. Through the haze of half-consciousness, he tried to lift himself up. The strength had gone from his body though, and he couldn't move so much as his arm.

'I'm over here,' he called out, but wasn't surprised that only a squeak came from his mouth.

Enid was smiling. She had seen him. She was coming over. No, she wasn't looking at him, but past him to somebody else. He thought it was one of the nurses. She was probably going to thank them for all their help. Rennison tried to twist round, but the pain in his body had redoubled. The merest twitch of his head brought back the huge invisible weight pressing down on his chest and the irregular thumping of his heart grew louder and louder, filling his entire head. He turned his eyes. Enid had her arms outstretched. She had Sugden in her arms. Rennison's eyes filled with tears. He couldn't speak or attract their attention in any other way. They embraced. She was whispering to him. He was nodding. Even before she produced the little box with the ring from her pocket, Rennison knew what she was saying. The accumulated lifetime of intimacies Rennison wanted to whisper to Enid would have overshadowed every one of those novels he had read all those years ago. It was too late. His mouth opened like a goldfish, but no sound came out. At the very moment when he realised the true identity of the intended victim, the intolerable weight on his chest eased. His last consciousness was the light-headed thought that his heart wasn't crashing about wildly in his chest like a pendulum any more. In the last few seconds of this Leap Year day, it had stopped.

JOHN BAKER

(Photo: Anna Baker)

John Baker is the author of the Sam Turner novels, set in York, and published by Gollancz. Three novels, POET IN THE GUTTER, DEATH MINUS ZERO, and KING OF THE STREETS are currently available, and the fourth, WALKING WITH GHOSTS, is scheduled for publication early in 1999. Work will begin next year on a TV version of POET IN THE GUTTER.

After living in Norway and France, he has now settled in York, where he lives with his wife and family.

John Baker

MILLENNIUM

A CITY BLUES

Church bells.

Sam Turner's eyes snapped open. This wasn't Sunday morning in Rome. The last Sunday morning he'd spent in Rome had been three years earlier in '97, and then he'd opened his eyes to a blue sky and a soft mattress. There'd been a warm presence beside him in the bed, fair hair spilled on the pillow. A smell of toasted almonds and coconut.

This was different. In place of the mattress was the wooden staircase up to his office. His chin was on one of the steps, his shoulder on another, and the rest of him was quilted backwards as far as he could imagine. Something moved close to his right eye, and he saw it was his hand, flecked with crusted blood. He moved it again, voluntarily, until the pain in his shoulder and chest made him stop. The smell of his sweat and dirt from the treads filled his nostrils. He closed his eyes and concentrated on the bells. Great Peter, rich and sonorous, trying to express something unknowable from its lofty chamber in the heights of the York Minster bell tower.

A memory surfaced. Sam had been scheduled to talk to a combined meeting of the Rotary and Inner Wheel at the Viking Moat House. His subject, A Day In The Life Of A Private Eye. The original speaker, the one who had cancelled at the last minute, had been booked to speak on the millennium, a topical subject, as the event itself was due in 21 days. Sam was the replacement speaker. He'd been seeing flashes of yellow all that morning, hallucinating grey worms and shrunken skulls. He'd arrived at the venue a couple of hours early and had his first drink in one year, seven months, three weeks, five days, and six hours. During that time he'd listened to a small voice inside his head every day: the voice that told him he didn't want a drink. But that particular day the voice was smaller than usual, and Sam wasn't listening.

He looked at the tumbler of scotch on the bar for some time without touching it. One drink wasn't gonna hurt. Might even get him through the lunch. He put the glass to his nose and took a whiff, stuck the tip of his tongue into the spirit, and finally put the glass back down on the bar. Pushed it away.

Then he drank it in one and asked the barman for a refill. 'Call it a death wish if you like,' Sam said with a grin. But the barman was too young to be friendly with someone who didn't fit. Sam sipped the second drink. Half way through the third he settled down to watch the people arriving for the lunch. The Chief Constable came in, together with his wife. He was a thin man with a long thin face, and she kept in step with him, remained close whenever he moved. They were reputedly a happy couple. Sam had another sip of his drink. Even among the middle classes faint traces of a monogamic instinct sometimes survives.

Sam's bank manager came into the room, looked at Sam and walked out again. He was the kind of guy who'd lend you his umbrella when the sun was shining and want it back the minute it began to rain. He returned surrounded by a group of fat-cat lawyers and solicitors. The kind of people who could, if Sam played his cards right, keep him in business for the rest of his life. He turned and smiled at each of them. Raised his glass in a silent salute. But they were suddenly very busy seeing to their ladies.

The chairman arrived, a man old enough to have been a waiter at the Last Supper. His face was a sea of wrinkles. His eyes like tiny black shells. He spoke with a West Country accent, modified by a lifetime in the north. 'My name is Roger Lame. We're so glad you could come. Everyone is excited about it.'

Lame? As he was ushered through to the dining room Sam told himself it would be cheap to make a joke about the guy's name.

At the top table he was introduced to the chairlady of the Inner Wheel, a woman who might have been pretty enough to hold up a game of darts around the time of the Second World War. The Lord Mayor was there, together with two prospective parliamentary candidates, and the society editors of the Yorkshire Post and Yorkshire Life. The room was seething with them, the top people of the town, sloshing back cocktails, making funny handshakes, and getting it on in the crude and inimitable way that the rich and far-too-comfortable have made their own. Like a group of people who had been individually kicked in the head by their ponies when they were children, and now believe everything they read in the papers.

Sam looked away, but the view was the same whichever way you came at it. They were spread out around him like a carpet of mould. When the waiter arrived, Lame asked Sam if he wanted a drink, and if the guy hadn't been so old and frail Sam'd've given him a good old thump on the back. 'Tell you what?' he said. 'Get me a scotch. On second thoughts, make it a double. No, two doubles.' Lame looked back to check it wasn't a joke, and Sam gave him the twinkle he'd stolen from Paul Newman twenty years earlier. Lame turned it all over in what he was pleased to call his mind, and worked it out from that one twinkle that there was no joke involved. To put the guy at ease, Sam added: 'I don't normally drink, just getting ready for the millennium.' The waiter and chairman exchanged glances, and seven minutes later, Sam had two glasses in front of him, each of them containing the amber liquid.

He forced himself to eat the chicken and the roast potatoes, suspecting he would see little solid nourishment in the build-up to the great day. He decided to abandon his prepared speech, and after the meal he had the two glasses refilled in front of him. When the chairman had finished his introduction Sam got to his feet. He downed one of the glasses and began to speak. 'Seen a comet in the sky last night. And it reminded me of you.' He grinned at them, and three of them grinned back. Two lies in one breath, but why not butter them up a little? Tell them anything. 'It's been a horrific century hasn't it? The conflicts of our time, too numerous to mention in an hour: I'm not even gonna try. Big wars, little wars; massacres, systematic and random. And that's before we begin to think about the environment. I wanted to mention these things. I know I'm here to talk about private detectives, but this millennium thing is steaming up behind us real fast now, and I wanna get it in perspective. Seems to me we have at least as much to regret as we have to celebrate.'

Sam put the remaining glass to his lips and sent the scotch on its way. He held the empty glass at a slight angle and looked sideways at the chairman. No help there, the guy was all buttoned up in an impenetrable little coat of complacency. Sam turned to the waiter who was standing at the back of the room, and drew him forward with his eyes. 'Same again,' he said. 'And keep them coming.'

He fixed his eyes on a lady JP who was unfortunately endowed with the kind of mamilla that a seasoned Friesian heifer would give her eye teeth for. He gave the remainder of his speech to her. Something about marriage, Alcoholics Anonymous, and Renaissance man.

He brought his bloody hand back into focus in the gloom of the stairwell. He remembered when he was small and he had to look after his cousin. Lucyboots didn't always remember to have a wee when she needed one, and it was Sam's job to remind her. He learned to pick up on the signs. She would start off fidgeting, moving her legs around, jumping up and down on the spot. From time to time she'd stop and push both hands down between her legs.

If he missed that stage, or didn't actually stand over her and make her do it, she'd go into stage two, which was where she'd cross her legs and make sucking sounds with her lips. That was what you might call stage critical.

The young Sam wasn't old enough to do the job. Lucyboots wet herself more times than he was able to stop her, and he was always in trouble for it because he should have reminded her in time. One day he'd washed her knickers in the pond and dried them in the sun. But he was still in trouble because the grown-ups could smell what had happened.

Another whisky hit the spot. There was a bishop at the table to Sam's left, a man who'd seen the light, a ticket-tout outside the gates of heaven. A heap of chicken bones in front of him. The clergyman whispered something to a woman sitting next to him who looked as though her soul had got the better of her.

The air was damp with well-bred distress.

When the world was young and everyone in it merely children Sam Turner had been in a crowded meeting room somewhere near Nelson's Column with Alfie Bass and Phil Ochs and Vanessa Redgrave. All the chairs were taken, and people were standing at the back of the room. Phil Ochs had thrown a wobbly. Oh, sure, he was against the Vietnam War, but he didn't think communism was the answer. He sang a beautiful and passionate rock'n'roll version of 'Flower Lady' which reminded some of the people in the room that they were human. Ochs didn't hang around to see the effect he'd created. He had a date with destiny, and not a lot of time on his hands. Later Vanessa and Alfie and Sam went to a Chinese restaurant and ate crispy duck and noodles. They drank scented tea, steaming hot. Vanessa and Sam, and Alfie, they thought they were gonna stop the Vietnam war. But they miscalculated. It would take an enormous American body count, and a new generation of economists before the warriors put their guns away.

Phil Ochs and Alfie were both dead now.

The bells were still ringing when Sam got up on his elbow. Both of his legs were numb, but he flexed his toes, then his ankles, and slowly the blood began pumping life back into his body.

He'd gone to Hull after the Rotary meeting. There'd been no questions after his speech, and he didn't hang around in the bar. It wasn't possible to·drink in York, there were too many people to stop him. But he wasn't known in Hull.

A three week drunk.

The old man in the tank hadn't been able to understand the difference between Donna and Dora. Two women Sam had loved and lost. One to a hit-and-run driver, and the other to cancer. 'Donna, Dora,' the old man'd said. 'Dorna Nobis.' And they'd sung it together. Dor-na, No-bis, pacem, pacem, Do-o-rna Nobis pa-a-acem, Do-o-o-orna-a No-o-bis pacem. . .

The bells were not going to stop ringing. Sam got to his knees and discovered the woman's leg a little higher up the stairs. Two legs, connected to a body that was cold and had no pulse. He shivered. He couldn't make out her face in the gloom, but he knew it was no one he'd ever met. It felt like a set-up, as if someone really didn't like Sam Turner. He got to his feet, swayed on the step, then found his balance. Things to sort out here. Time to go to work. He wouldn't have a drink today. Might never drink again.

The church bells were pealing out all over York - all over the world - but the sun hadn't come up. It was still dark. Sam Turner and a corpse and the morning of a new millennium. Felt like days of old. Familiar ring to it.

An old enemy setting him up? The police? Something unthought of? Or was it just God again?

ROBERT BARNARD

Robert Barnard was born in 1936, and grew up in Brightlingsea, near Colchester, in Essex. After Balliol College (1956-9) he worked for a year with the Fabian Society, then went to Australia as a lecturer in English at the University of New England, NSW (which he used in his first crime novel, *Death Of An Old Goat*). He married in 1963. In 1966 he came back to Europe, to lecture at the University of Bergen in Western Norway, where he took a doctorate, with a thesis on Dickens, in 1972. In 1976 he became Professor of English at the world's most northerly university, Tromsø, in North Norway, where he stayed until he went full time as a writer in 1983.

His first crime novel was published in 1974, and since then he has written over thirty. He has also written books on Dickens, Agatha Christie and a *Short History of English Literature* for Blackwells.

Robert Barnard

DIVINE ANGER

"**I** say, it isn't, is it?—It couldn't be.—Jessey?—Antony Jessey?"
Bill Flack had turned round as he finished signing the hotel register and had
begun to reach down for his suitcase when there was this face, this face from his
past. Older, much older, but a face vividly remembered. For Bill had a memory for
faces, quite apart from particular reasons for remembering.

The man smiled back at him uncertainly.

"I don't quite—Wait a minute. Flack! Good Lord! Was it Jim? Jim Flack?"

"Bill. Well, well, well. What brings you here? You can't be part of the conference,
surely? It must be—what?—twenty-five years since—"

But it seemed like only yesterday. That succession of long hot days in the summer
of 'sixty-four. His friends around the council estate all seemed to be away: a week in
Blackpool, day trips to Scarborough or "Brid," even one—greatly daring—on a
family holiday in Marbella. Only he, Bill Flack, still in Leeds. His father had lost his
job on the brewery lorry two months before, and his mother was working part-time
in the local baker's shop to supplement the dole. No holiday or even day trip for the
Flacks that year. His father was short-tempered and bored out of his mind. His
mother was harassed.

They had met by the canal. Bill went there quite a lot with his rod and line to
escape from the pressures of the family home. If you were going to be lonely, fishing
was a nice thing to be lonely doing. There were quite a few, young and old, dotted
along the canal bank, but they seldom swapped more than a few words. Yorkshire
fishermen were among the dourest of a dour breed. Antony had been out walking
and had stopped behind him, looking over his shoulder. Bill had registered that they
were of an age, about fifteen, and that Antony was very much better dressed than he.
Such things were conspicuous at Bill's grammar school. He had smiled briefly at
the stranger and gone back to watching his line.

"Do you catch anything much?"

The voice was conspicuously well bred, with not a trace of Yorkshire or Leeds in
it. It was friendly, however, and unpatronizing. Bill shrugged.

"Sometimes."

"I mean, big enough to eat?"

"Now and then. Mostly it's tiddlers, stuff for the cat.—Like to sit and hold it?"

Antony nodded. He sat there holding the rod in a wonderfully steady hand. Bill
crouched on his haunches on the canal path beside him and they talked—hesitantly,
conscious of a gap between them at first, but still they talked.

Antony had just come back from a family holiday in Austria. He had been rather bored. He lived in a large Victorian house two minutes from Bill's council estate. He had no friends in the area because he went to a boarding school in Derbyshire. "Massingham. It's not a *public* school. It's no great shakes," he explained apologetically. "I wouldn't board there if I had the choice. Where do you go?"

Bill jerked his head toward the grammar school on the hill above them. "It's not bad. At least I live at home. Though me dad's out of work and everybody's a bit — tensed up."

Antony nodded as if he understood. Bill wondered if he did. Then the line jerked, and Bill helped him land a fish—not a large one, but something bigger than a tiddler. Antony smiled at him, obviously pleased.

"Will you be here tomorrow?" he asked before he walked on, and Bill nodded.

It was after the second day of their acquaintanceship that they walked home together via Antony's house. They were talking and it just seemed to happen that way. Bill knew the houses, of course, but they had always seemed to him something remote, something other. They stood outside the front gate and Bill tried not to stare: a stone house, with an impressive bay, and three storeys. What did they do with all that space, Bill wondered.

"Will you come in?" Antony asked politely. Bill shook his head.

"Me mam will be back from the shop," he said obscurely. As he walked away he felt he had been boorish, and he turned and shouted:

"See you tomorrow!"

After four or five sessions Antony thought he was getting the hang of fishing. It was a pleasant activity, but not all-absorbing. He tried again.

"Why don't you come round to our house tomorrow?" he asked. "There's a lot of space at the back. I'm practising bowling."

Cricket was of absorbing interest to Bill. He hesitated only for a fraction of a second before nodding.

He went round next afternoon about two. Mrs. Jessey was on her way out, to a meeting of a charity committee. From a vantage point of twenty-five years later, Bill could characterize her as "early Oxfam." She was pleasant, uncondescending, but dauntingly well dressed.

"There's some buttered scones on the kitchen table," she said, putting on her hat in front of the hall mirror. "They're homemade, and not bad."

Bill could not envisage her flushed from cooking in the kitchen, as his mother always was. Perhaps she had a woman in to do it. The boys went through to the back garden—a large rectangular lawn bordered by roses, hydrangeas, and shrubs Bill did not know the names of. There were stumps set up at the far end, and a bat lying on the grass.

"It seems funny not to be in white," said Antony, taking up the ball. "Will you bat?"

It didn't seem funny at all to Bill not to be in white. But he enjoyed the practice. Antony was a formidably good bowler, but he himself was no mean bat. Sometimes he had to be very careful not to hit out. He was afraid of breaking a window in that gracious house. When they swapped round, Antony proved as incompetent with the bat as Bill was with the ball. They gave up, laughing. As they were going back into the house through the back door, Bill caught sight of a gleaming new racing bike leaning against the side of the house. Antony saw him looking, but said nothing about it. He was suddenly embarrassed by his possessions.

When they had collected the scones and a bottle of Coca-Cola, they went up to Antony's room—that was one use of a three-storey house, thought Bill—and they said nothing about the mass of prestigious toys, games, and gear scattered around the large Victorian bedroom: the table football, the new rugby boots, the electric train set, the roller-skates and ordinary skates, the snorkel set. They sat and talked, with a new sort of awkwardness—talked about the forthcoming General Election, about schoolwork, what they liked and didn't like, what they would do at GCE and whether they would stay on afterwards. When they were finished with the scones, Bill thought it was silly not to mention anything in the room, so he asked about the table football.

"I haven't played much," said Antony, with a shrug of indifference, but getting up to demonstrate. "It was a silly present, really, because all my friends are at school, not around here. You go down that end—"

They played, but their hearts weren't in it. Afterwards, Antony asked casually if Bill could roller-skate. Bill had never tried, but they compared feet and found them much of a size, and they went down to the paved path and tarmac square in front of the garage and Antony taught Bill. That was more fun, even though it did involve a lot of falling down.

"There's a rink out at Meeston," said Antony. "You can rent the skates." He nearly added: "It's quite cheap," but saved himself in time.

They were standing by the back door, and Bill began getting ready to go home. "Mam likes us all to be home for tea when she gets back from work," he explained. "She's got a lot to do."

Antony nodded, oddly awkward again.

"Will your father get a job soon?" he asked.

"I suppose so. He's lost jobs in the past and always found one again."

"There's plenty of jobs around," agreed Antony.

Why something should have snapped in Bill at that, he himself never knew. Something quite irrational, some divine anger, caught hold of him and he swung round.

"You mean there's plenty of jobs of the sort my dad can do, don't you?"

"No! No—of course I didn't!"

"You mean there's plenty of labouring jobs that a working-class thicky like him can pick up—"

"I don't! I don't know your dad!"

"I've had you up to *here* with your cricket whites and your skates and your—"

The wave of rage and frustration overwhelmed him, and he threw himself on the boy, pummelling his head, banging it against the wall, and kicking him with a vicious desperation. Then he ran, choking with rage and self-disgust, out of the gate and down the leafy road towards his home.

Later a policeman called round. Knowing the sort of people the Jesseys probably were, he had guessed that was what would happen. They would prefer to deal through the police. When the constable was led into the front room, Bill was flushed and bitterly ashamed. He burst into tears, and all he could say through his sobs was: "He was so bloody tactful!" It sounded silly even to himself. The policeman was avuncular and thought he understood the problem, and he made Bill promise he would write Antony a letter of apology, which he did—a stilted, schoolboyish letter through which there showed a genuine shame.

Now they were standing, still awkward together, in the foyer of the Royal Hotel, Scarborough.

"Well, well, well," said Bill, who could not rid himself of a slight feeling that this was an unlucky meeting. "Are you really with the conference? I had no idea you were in computers."

"I wasn't until three or four years ago. I'm a latecomer—like most."

"That's right. I was immensely lucky being in on the ground floor. I say: I've just had an idea. Are you going to the president's shindig tonight?"

"Well, I had thought to—"

"Give it a miss. They're always deadly, and the current president's got about as much savoir faire as a groundhog. Come and have a sherry in my room, and then we can forage for dinner somewhere or other. My wife's off out—she's up there changing now. She has a school reunion, by an odd coincidence. I married a Yorkshire lass, in a way, you see."

The would-be homely phrase came out unnaturally. Somehow it seemed they would never be at ease with each other. Antony wished he could refuse the invitation, but the burden of those days so many years ago sat heavy on him.

"That would be very pleasant," he said.

"Right. It's Room 407. Say in an hour's time? We've got a lot to make up for."

He had meant to say, "We've got a lot of time to make up," but that wasn't how it had come out.

Room 407, when Antony went there a tactful five minutes late, was in reality a suite. All the hotel was splendid, in a post-Regency way, but this suite must have been one of the best there. The furniture was repro-stately-home, and there were original pictures by local artists on the walls. Bill's wife was called Penny: she was beautiful, friendly, and on her way out.

"So nice to meet one of Bill's old friends," she said, a bit breathless. "We don't get to Leeds any more since Bill's parents died—It *is* going to be an evening of school reminiscences, isn't it?"

So Bill had not told her the situation.

"Drink?"

Bill went over to a side table, on which stood a large array of bottles supplied by the hotel.

"Golly, what a choice! You must be expecting to entertain."

"Oh—you know: competitors and customers. Now that I'm vice-chairman, it goes with the job. And you never know: Penny may come back with some old school pals. Though I don't think so: it was one of those rigid, authoritarian private schools that aroused either devotion or aversion. In Penny's case, it was rather the latter. It was only the coincidence of our being here anyway that persuaded her to go to the reunion. Now, what'll it be?"

"A dry sherry would be fine."

"We educate our kids locally," continued Bill, pouring. 'I mean locally in London. Penny is a Hampshire girl, and she hated being away from home—as you did, I seem to remember. Luckily we're not starved for choice of schools, and we picked good ones for ours. A good cricketing school for the boys," he added, smiling as he handed over the drink.

Antony smiled, a little more relaxed. "I still support Yorkshire," he said. "Though it's not the team it was."

"You can say that again!" Bill sat down on the sofa and gave his full attention to his guest. "Well, how come we've never met before at these jamborees? I've been coming—heavens!—seventeen years. Ever since I joined English Electronics."

So he was vice-chairman of English Electronics—a very large, prosperous, prestigious firm in the computer world. It was a job in a million, and no doubt paid accordingly.

Oh—I'm a Johnny-come-lately in the business," said Antony deprecatingly. "I'm only here because my boss went down with flu. I'm mightily impressed by your job. No doubt I've seen your name often enough and never made the connection."

"Some things are best pushed to the back of the mind." Bill smiled, feeling less awkward now that it was out in the open. "God! What a fool I was. The sooner you forgot about *that* the better. As for the job, I was lucky. I had a few years with ICI after university, then I decided that I'd rather be a larger fish in a smaller pond. I was in on the ground floor with English Electronics, so I had a head start."

"And now you're a big fish in a big pond."

"As it's turned out," agreed Bill.

"I've always wished I'd gone to university," said Antony.

"Didn't you?"

"I had a place," said Antony bleakly. "At Oxford. Then my dad fell ill. Parkinson's Disease. Of course it was the beginning of the end for him, though it took a long, long while. He wanted me to take over the business."

"I don't think you ever told me what your dad did," said Bill apologetically.

"A chain of electrical shops in Leeds and Bradford. Quite a nice little concern—I got a reasonable sum for it when I sold up."

"Oh—you made me a pile and moved on, did you?"

"Well, not a pile. Business hadn't been all that wonderful. I hadn't my dad's flair, or authority. And then there was a divorce settlement that took a lot of it."

Bill looked down into his glass. "Oh, I was wondering whether you were married. I *am* sorry. Though these days, it's so common, you have to think to count up the marriages that *have* survived. I'm just grateful that Penny can stand the pace and stand the life. Benign neglect—that's what she describes our married life as. I'm going to retire early and make it up to her."

Antony smiled uncertainly.

"It wasn't really like that with us." He stood up and began walking round the sitting room of Bill's suite. "Anthea wasn't neglected—I was never that involved with my work. I think the marriage died of boredom. There were no children, you see. We did both want children. Failing that, I think Anthea would have settled for an exciting life; or a glamorous one even. But that's not really Leeds, is it? She filled her life in various ways—took over some of Mother's charity work, that sort of thing, but it didn't help with her own—emptiness, her own hunger. In the end, the marriage just fell apart. She moved out. We run into each other now and then, meet for dinner. We've even talked of going on holiday together again. But we find we haven't got anything much to say to each other."

His voice faded into silence.

"I'm sorry," said Bill again.

"At least I have the job."

"That's right," said Bill heartily. "That gives you an interest."

"It fills in the time, anyway. I think if I had my time over I'd do something entirely different. History, for example. I dabble in local history, but I haven't really got the method—I do a lot of reading, too."

"I just don't seem to have the time for reading," said Bill, and then regretted it.

"Of course you wouldn't. Take a nice fat book with you when you go on holiday—I imagine that's about it with you, isn't it?"

Bill smiled, all the old awkwardness back, and nodded.

"That's natural, with your work, and your family. But I read a lot. It fills in the time, and keeps the mind occupied. I sometimes feel I'm in danger of letting my mind go a complete blank and staying that way. Luckily, I don't much like television. That really *would* be giving up." He was still walking restlessly about the room.

"Haven't you got enough money from the sale of the firm to make a fresh start?" Bill asked. "Do something you really want to do?"

There was silence. When Antony's voice started again it was clear that he hadn't heard. The voice was somehow disembodied, like the voice of a penitent reaching a priest in the confessional.

"They gave me the job out of charity, of course. I suppose you guessed that. I had plenty of contacts, so when things fell apart Airedale Electronics turned up trumps. They're a small firm, but I do my best for them. I wish my heart was in it. I have a small bungalow in Guiseley. No point in anything bigger. I do for myself—cook, clean, all that."

Bill wondered whether to say again that he was sorry. He thought not, but could think of nothing else to say.

"My life is empty!"

The bitterness cut through the stale air of the room. It was a cry of pain. Bill shifted in his seat. Something had to be said.

"I think I know how you feel, old chap." He looked around the room, his suite. "I think, you know, you feel something like I did when—"

He didn't finish. He felt the force of the man as he threw himself at the sofa, felt the hands around his neck. The thought flashed through his mind that justice

29

demanded he make no resistance. The hands circled his throat—strong, bowler's hands, he remembered—and then they squeezed tighter and tighter. Bill's last thought before the darkness engulfed him was how to suggest, tactfully, that honours were now even.

PETER CROWTHER

(Photo: Seamus A. Ryan)

Primarily known for his anthologies and his collaborative novel with James Lovegrove (ESCARDY GAP), Peter Crowther has some 70 published stories to his credit (mainly in the US, where most are set), including many mystery tales and a whole series featuring New York private eye Koko Tate. Here, in the first of a projected series that's set a little closer to his home town of Harrogate, he turns his attention to the fictional Calder Valley town of Luddersedge and an engaging tale of home-grown murder.

Peter Crowther

THE ALLOTMENT

Perhaps the only person in Luddersedge who hadn't known that Maureen Walker was fed up to the back teeth of her husband Stanley was Stan himself. But then there were many things that life, in its infinite and capricious wisdom, blew past Stan's eyes and even right under his nose... just like the tick-tock, tell-the-time dandelion seeds forever airborne around the hummocks and holes of Stan's beloved allotment.

It wouldn't be fair to say that Stan didn't care for Maureen, although to suggest that he actually loved her possibly stretched the truth a jot. He cared for her in his very own special way, even though she wasn't the be-all and end-all of his life (she did turn out to be one of those, but that's jumping the gun a little).

The truth was that the two things which probably came closest to earning Stan Walker's affection — aside from his allotment — were (a) watching football on the TV and (b) the Black Sheep brewery up in Masham, to whose continued financial success and security Stan had contributed more than his share over the years.

Stan's only other weakness was a seemingly endless stream of ideas for how he and Maureen could get-rich-quick, such as the specialist sweet shop in Todmorden or the mobile Dating Agency he set up in Rochdale: Stan was always promising his wife that the next one would be The Big One — that once-in-a-lifetime golden opportunity to make money — but each scheme had come and gone with little to show for its passing but another hole in their meagre savings.

All of these were thorns in Maureen's side but, in aggravation terms, it was the allotment that took the biscuit.

The allotment — one of six in a standalone patch of land on Honeydew Lane, edging onto the lane itself as well as onto Smithfield Road, Carholme Place and Carholme Drive — was an 80-square yards rectangle of vegetable-festooned soil interspersed with narrow grassy 'tending' paths. The allotment's main border, Honeydew Lane, one of the town's primary vehicular arteries and site of the notorious Bentley's Tannery, was an area blighted by such permanently pungent fumes that (or so local legend had it) the infamous Hounds of Luddersedge — an itinerant canine pack of all shapes and sizes (though mostly of a common variety: Heinz 57) given to defecating on the pavements of the town — were drawn to the locality, frequently depositing turds of varying consistency in and around the carefully and even lovingly cultivated plants and produce.

It was here that Stan spent increasing amounts of his time. Since he retired early (aged 52, now some four years ago) from the buses (a mobile and carefree life wandering the lanes between Rochdale and Burnley and Halifax), he had spent the hours and days and weeks (not to mention months, seasons and years) dreaming of The Big One — the idea that would make them their millions (or at least a few thousands) — and tending his prided potatoes crop.

There had been a time, in the late fifties, when the young Stan had gone to help his father every Sunday morning, when the streets of Luddersedge had been an olfactory grotto of the smells of Yorkshire pudding-mix and quietly cooking joints of meat and pans of vegetables, and the allotments had been well-tended and picturesque. But those were the old days. Now, two of the other five allotments had gone to weed and a third one, Maureen had noticed one day when she walked down to the shops, was already showing signs of neglect. Stan would regularly come home looking glum because he'd found half-squashed empty beer cans jammed in amongst his sweetpeas... and, on one occasion, a used condom beside a flattened section of potato plants.

"Some folk'll do it anywhere," Stan announced on his return from that particular Sunday visit to the allotment, wafting straight to the sports pages of *The News Of The World* as he sat waiting for his dinner. "I don't know what's happening to the world, I really don't."

Serving the mashed potato out onto her best blue-flowered plates using an ice cream scoop bought for her at the massive Ikea warehouse on an all-too-infrequent outing to Leeds by Stan for her birthday, Maureen quietly but fervently wished that her husband might introduce a similar element of adventure and spontaneity into their own lovelife. At 53, and still in the prime of her life (as she delighted in telling anyone who would listen), Maureen Walker craved some excitement. The truth was she craved anything at all that would break the humdrum life she had somehow drifted into without even seeing it coming towards her. But such was not to be the case.

Stan Walker was not an adventurous man. Nor was he spontaneous, affectionate, interesting, learned, amusing, successful or (much as Maureen didn't even like to think it) handsome. And while her husband had probably never been any of these things even when he was running around the streets and lanes of Luddersedge in his short trousers, playing hide-and-seek or looking for conkers in the cool autumns of the Calder Valley, Maureen firmly placed the blame for her current situation at but one door: the allotment.

As far as Maureen Walker was concerned, it was the allotment that was the villain of the piece... and so it was, on one of those lonely, empty summer mornings when Stan had already left the house, that the arrival of an official-looking letter from the local council provided her with what she considered to be a neat solution to her problem.

Maureen used to joke — though somewhat without humour even at the beginning — in those days when the pair went out together of an evening, usually down to the Conservative Club on Eldershot Road but more often to The Three Pennies public house on Pennypot Drive where Stan could get his fix of Black Sheep, that Stan's 'other woman' was a piece of ground filled with cabbages and carrot-tops. It used to get a laugh for a time, from whoever might be sitting with them... and even from Maureen herself, though Stan would never respond. He would simply throw an occasional nod into the conversation, a distant half-smile on his face that suggested he had been drugged or was merely pulling out of a long coma into a world that he neither recognised nor cherished. And all the while he would repeatedly lift the ever-present pint glass of Masham's finest for a series of life-renewing slurps.

Unable to get much out of her husband, Maureen took to laying it on the line as far as her home-life went with anyone who would take the time to listen — and as far as Luddersedge went, that was a lot of people.

Maureen would bemoan her lot to Joan Cardew and Miriam Barrett — of numbers 10 and 14 respectively — over the rickety fence that separated her and Stan's house from Joan's and Eddie's and the shock of privet that formed an unkempt but effective barrier with the widowed Mrs Barrett's threadbare patch of grass.

With clothes hung freshly out to dry in the wind blowing through the Calder Valley — predominantly Stan's voluminous Y-fronts and Maureen's no-longer-very-lacy bras and pants from Marks and Sparks — Maureen would, at one time... in the early days, tell either Joan or Miriam that she was nearing the end of her tether. That if he didn't leave her then she would take the bull by the horns and leave him.

She would tell the same thing to lisping Bert Green at the greengrocer's on the High Street, as Bert watched her pressing the sides of his avocados with undisguised annoyance; and to young Kylie Bickershaw with the bitten-down fingernails who worked the checkout at the Netto's behind the Station car park and seemed to make a habit of short-changing everyone; and even to Billy Roberts, the quiffed and always-tanned would-be gigolo who carved a mean rack of chops in his father's butcher's shop at the corner of Lemon Road and Coronation Drive.

Sometimes, when Maureen was watching young Billy — some thirty years her junior — carve a joint or pound beefsteak, it was all she could do to keep from openly drooling... watching those biceps work, and those thighs balloon out to fill his tight, black trousers. One time, when he caught her and saw the naked desire on her face, Billy said, "Looks to me you could pop it into your mouth right here, Mrs. Walker," and Maureen readily agreed, blushing faintly at the idea that Billy might well have read her thoughts... not one of which had anything to do with meat (at least, none of the stuff being turned around on Billy's slab). Needless to say, Billy knew that just as well as Maureen did.

And so it was that word spread around Luddersedge the way it will spread around any small town, sometimes reaching the far end before the person who set it off even gets there. Not that Maureen actually wanted everyone to know her business — she didn't. It was simply a release valve and, anyway, subconsciously, she considered service people and neighbours to be the souls of discretion — but, of course, things don't always work out the way we intend them. And when a release valve becomes blocked, the pressure has to escape somewhere.

"I hear things aren't so good with you and your Stan," Mary Connaught said to Maureen one day, groaning with relief as she switched the straining net carrier bag from her welt-disfigured left hand into the right. "Is it that you're getting sick of waiting for The Big One?"

Maureen decided to ignore the remark about Stan's schemes — 'treat it with the contemp it dizzerbs,' her mother would have said in her characteristic pigeon-English dialect. "Whoever told you that?" she asked, feigning surprise and even a dose of healthy indignation, one hand lifted to fiddle with the cameo brooch that Maureen's Auntie Lillian had bequeathed to her the previous year and the other laid spread-fingered on her hip.

Mary Connaught shrugged. "A little bird," she said.

The confidante in question was neither a bird nor was it little. It was, in fact, Jim Fairclough with whom Mary had been having something of a hot-and-sweaty flirtation since the departure of Mary's husband Thomas — Thomas having fled the family nest not only with the contents of his and Mary's joint account at the building society over in Hebden Bridge (amounting to some £16,000 when interest had been added) but also with the cashier who served him to boot. The pair were said to be now living in Ibiza — where Thomas and Mary had spent their summer holidays for their entire married life of eight-getting-on-nine years ("... adding insult to injury," was how Miriam Barrett had summed it up... an opinion undoubtedly echoed by Mary) — and, for a time, Mary had considered trying to track them down. But then she started the relationship with Jim and all other things just kind of got pushed to the back of her mind.

Jim Fairclough's brother Martin was a regular feature wherever Billy Roberts appeared — there were some about town who said the two of them were like one person and that person's shadow, though who was which was a debatable point — and so Mary had heard all about Maureen's looks and the perspiration that always appeared on her top lip while Billy was pounding his meat. She heard about them on Jim's now frequent visits to her house — always under cover of darkness... though that did not matter a jot to Harriet Williams, the eagle-eyed sentinel of number 41 (Mary's house was number 43) who, in turn, was spreading the news to any who would stop and listen — while Jim had fun with the split-crotch panties he had bought for her from a small shop on Brewer Street during a day-trip excursion to London to watch Jim's beloved Burnley play away to Watford. (All things considered, the purchase was something of a selfish present on Jim's part although, if she were to be truthful, Mary would have to confess to getting a healthier degree of enjoyment out of wearing it than she derived from any of her other undergarments.)

The conversation drifted to other things — a move started with Maureen's wide-eyed and innocent enquiry whether Mary had heard anything from her errant husband — and then pulled to a close with both women suddenly remembering other places they had arranged to be.

As Maureen watched Mary Connaught walk purposefully across the road, pausing only to give a wave to Pete Dickinson in his customised Cortina (Pete was the mechanic at Tony Manderson's garage over on Eldershot Road), she realised just how incestuous Luddersedge really was. It shouldn't really have taken her so long: after all, Miriam Barrett had said once that you couldn't break wind in Luddersedge without folks stopping you in the street to ask if you were having tummy problems. But you rarely saw the whole picture when you were only one of the characters painted into the scene.

However, there were other things that the momentous encounter with Mary Connaught brought to the fore: the main one of these was that Maureen could go on no longer talking behind Stan's back. She frowned at this thought. *And why is that?* a small voice enquired from the deep recesses of her head.

Yes, why was that?

Maureen looked up at the stone buildings that hemmed her in, imagining the roads that lay beyond them — roads that led to other towns, other cities, even other countries — and she suddenly yearned for them and for the freedom to travel them, with the wind in her hair and not a care on her shoulders.

Mary Connaught reached the pavement at the other side of the road and looked determinedly in the Oxfam shop window.

And why couldn't she do that, Maureen wondered to herself — fully knowing the answer even before it came. Why couldn't she drift along the great Highway of Life with carefree abandon? Just one reason: Stan.

Exactly! said the small voice.

So why did she need to keep her own counsel after so many years of simply telling things the way they were?

Because, the small voice whispered (with Maureen suddenly realising that it was her own innermost thoughts given a kind of vocal substance), if she were going to get rid of him, she needed to appear in harmony with her husband in order to avoid attracting undue attention.

She was momentarily shocked. And then, slowly, a smile pulled at her mouth. The phrase 'get rid of' was somehow exciting... as if Stan was no more than a troublesome rash that needed only a spot of Clearasil to banish forever — and Maureen nodded to herself, watching Mary Connaught reach the double frontage of Luddersedge bakery and turn to give her a glance. Maureen waved, gave a big smile, and turned around, her back feeling straighter than it had done for some time.

A decision had been made... or, more accurately, acknowledged: it had actually been *made* a thousand trips to the allotment ago; a million snores ago; and a hundred unexciting and demeaning sessions of her husband's clammy and clumsy explorations of her body ago.

The truth was, indeed, out there: Stanley had to go.

And if he wasn't going to go of his own accord — which he clearly wasn't — well... then she would have to give him a helping hand.

Deciding to kill her husband after years of unconscious vacillation was like the sudden arrival last autumn at a decision to shift the sofa from against the back wall of the drawing room — where it had languished for as long as she could remember — over to beneath the window.

Complacency and a lack of adventure were the prime offenders and, just like it had been with the sofa, Maureen now saw lots of reasons why this was the obvious thing to do. More than that, it provided her with a frisson of excitement that had been missing from her life more or less since she and Stan had married in 1967.

The newspapers had called it the 'summer of love' — either that year or the one before or after: Maureen couldn't exactly recall which — but for the newlywed Walkers it had been the year of 'business pretty much as usual'. In other words, the spectacle of the panting, groaning figure of her husband (slimmer then, it had to be said, but still carrying a stone or so too much flesh) climbing on board the good ship Maureen for a quick launch before rolling over into a sleep promoted by Black Sheep and interspersed with raucous snoring.

The snoring had sometimes grown so loud that Maureen had taken to pinching her husband's buttocks between her fingernails to interrupt his slumber. It proved to be highly effective and — Maureen now realised in the flush of her decision to do away with her resident market-gardener (who now carried some four stones more than was ideal for his age and height) — it was strangely enjoyable in a kind of sadistic way.

So, there was the snoring: that would end; and there were the monosyllabic conversations in the Conservative Club or The Three Pennies — those would stop. And all the half-baked get-rich-quick schemes and the long-promised Big One that would keep them in clothespegs and manure for the rest of their empty lives. Not to mention, of course, the daily intake of Black Sheep, the constant loamy smell of earth and outdoors that Stan wafted in front of her when he deigned to return home for his food, and—worst of all she now realised — Stanley's occasional need to remove his striped pyjama bottoms and claim his conjugal rights while Maureen stared over his thrusting shoulders at the bedroom curtain blowing in the breeze from the open window... imagining, lying there with her legs spread wide, she was Tinkerbell in the Peter Pan story, preparing to fly off into the night and over the spires and sooty roofs of Luddersedge into a new and distant morning somewhere far away. Somewhere better.

Yes, it would be just like moving the sofa.

But how to do it was the question.

Eventually, having discounted garrotting and knifing (she didn't have a gun, so shooting was a non-starter), Maureen had almost lost hope — already starting to convince herself that the whole thing had been a pipe-dream... the naive whimsy of a bored housewife, like something out of a macabre version of Mills & Boon — when BBC2 ran a film about a hitman hired to murder the wife of a wealthy industrialist.

The film was complex — all the more so because Stan spent the entire duration of it slouched in the easy chair by her side snoring so loudly that she kept missing pieces of dialogue — but it was the basic principle that attracted her. For the first time in a long time, she felt randy — really randy: not the dull ache she got watching Billy Roberts but something almost primal... accentuated by the fact that Stan was right by her side, oblivious to the drama unfolding before his closed eyes.

"I'm going to do this to you," Maureen whispered, nodding toward the TV, her face bathed in the flickering glow of the screen on which a man stealthily crept around the outside of a house that, in Luddersedge, would have been a stately home. "I'm going to hire a hitman. What do you say to that?"

Stan snuffled and moved his head to one side before resuming his cacophonous drone.

The following day, with Stan already gone for a full session at the allotment, his pack-up of tuna-and-mayonnaise sandwiches in his little Tupperware container, Maureen did the dishes while she stared out of the window and wondered where she should go to hire someone to kill her husband.

Somehow, the prospect seemed daunting.

What went on in America — a fabled land that Maureen had never visited — seemed hard to translate in English terms. And even harder to translate in terms of Luddersedge.

It was like pop music, she mused, placing her favourite floral designed plate lovingly in the back of the draining rack beside the sink. Like '24 Hours From Tulsa' (she had always loved Gene Pitney) — you could never imagine it being '24 Hours From...': from where? Tottenham? It had to begin with a 'T' to preserve the alliteration (that wasn't how she thought of it, not knowing alliteration from an adverb, but she did recognise the need for a *tuh* sound to balance the one in '*tuh*wenty-four'). Torquay?

She sang the first line over the sound of Terry Wogan, while he rambled on about the DG in Auntie Beeb. "Own-lee, 24 hours from Tor-quay... own-lee one day away from your harms...' She chuckled and dropped cereal spoons and a butter knife into the holder, trailing suds across the crockery already drying.

It was comical but it was serious, too. It was serious because it was impossible... ridiculous and impossible. Where on earth could she find a hitman around Luddersedge... or even in the comparative metropolises of Halifax and Burnley and Bradford? The watery autumn sunshine through the kitchen windows was already making the whole idea seem a nonsense, the idle dream of a woman too long in one place and far too long in one relationship; a relationship which had spawned nothing but familiarity and indifference.

The answer came, as answers so often do, when Maureen was quietly but firmly prepared to abandon the problem that had called for it.

It came with the clatter of the post-box in the front door and the dull plop of something landing in the hallway, resounding so emphatically over the sound of the radio that Maureen half expected Terry Wogan to comment: *Well, listeners, let's find out what's in the 'Big Goody' that the postie's just dropped through the post-box of Luddersedge's very own Maureen Walker!*

The Big Goody in question was neither big nor good: it was only an update catalogue from Empire Stores. It lay on the mat with two letters at its base, looking briefly, for all the world, like a skull and crossbones. One of the letters, Maureen saw even as she stooped to pick them up, was a window envelope containing the gas bill. The other, a franked brown job, had Stan's name carefully typed in bold.

It was accepted in the Walker household that all post could be opened by whoever picked it off the mat in front of the door, no matter who it was addressed to. Thus it was that Maureen opened the official-looking letter that turned out to be from the local council.

The letter, from a clerk (of unknown gender and indecipherable signature) who went by the unlikely multi-syllabic name of S. Willingtonton (surely a typo), said in formal tones which oozed insincere regret that, as had been 'previously intimated', the 'allotment facility' in which Stan 'heretofore owned a one-sixth portion', was to be 'compulsorily withdrawn' and sold to a 'local consortium' for 'extensive redevelopment' by their (unnamed) client. Stan would be, S. Willingtonton continued, 'duly recompensed'. It closed with (a) a request for Stan to contact the Council offices as soon as possible and (b) the assurance that the author remained — 'sincerely' no less — Stan's.

She clutched the single sheet of paper in a quivering hand and smiled up at the ceiling.

Her husband's, beloved allotment was soon to be no more and he was about to become depressed. Very depressed. Moreover, though he did not yet know it, he was about to become suicidal.

Maureen had her hit man — it was Stanley himself.

The next day was a maelstrom of activity for the soon-to-be-widowed Maureen Walker, but then speed was essential.

Clearly, Stan could not be allowed to see the letter. Even a man as docile as Stanley Walker would be spurred to frenetic activity by the prospect of losing all that he held dear in life. Telephone calls would be made and, perhaps (God forbid), in the face of organised resistance on the part of the gardeners affected, the Council might even reconsider its decision.

The letter therefore duly disappeared into the labyrinthine recesses of Maureen's handbag, a shadowy and even hostile (being overtly feminine) terrain of mirrors and lipsticks and thick bandages with flyaway wings that Maureen inserted into her pants for a few days every month. It was a domain into which Stan seldom ventured unless pressed.

However, if Stan were to be rendered so uncharacteristically distraught, Maureen reasoned that the letter from S. Willingtonton — effectively her husband's suicide note — could not realistically be sat upon for too long. For the scenario she had concocted to work, he must receive it and he must take action immediately, while the balance of his mind was on the blink (or whatever they usually said in such cases).

41

Poison was the answer. And, with Stan's allotment shed undoubtedly containing all manner of suitable candidates for the job — slug pellets, greenfly sprays and other assorted insecticides — Maureen recognised an almost comical irony in the situation: an enemy for so long, the allotment was proving to be the means of her very salvation.

How to administer the answer to her prayers, however, posed something of a problem... but not for long. The solution, when it came, brought with it a pleasantly appropriate subtext: it would be in a healthy glass of Masham's finest. Stan would be put to rights by a Black Sheep.

Who done it? Maureen mused to herself as she sat in bed on the night of the fateful letter's arrival, with her husband happily snoring by her side oblivious to the trip he was about to make out of her life forever. *Ewe* done it!

It was all she could do to keep from laughing out loud. But she didn't think that would be either appropriate or fair: after all, letting him sleep undisturbed, even without the usual pinching of the fleshy pads masquerading as Stan's buttocks, was tantamount to a last meal. Let him enjoy it.

The small puzzle as to how Maureen might gain access to Stan's allotment shed without Stan being there was also neatly and unexpectedly solved the next morning when Stan announced over his breakfast that he wouldn't be needing his customary pack-up because he had to go into Leeds. Maureen didn't ask what the reason for this expedition might be: she didn't believe in looking a gift-horse in the mouth and, anyway, Stan occasionally made the trip to Leeds when something was needed for his allotment. (They had shops there that actually catered for the devoted gardener, their shelves replete with all manner of equipment and tools... not to mention a healthy supply of poisonous substances: Maureen hoped that Stan already had plenty of these in his shed.)

"Will you be coming straight back?" she asked, hardly daring to hope too much for the response she wanted. "I mean, do you want me to make you some sand- wiches for later in the afternoon?"

Stan shook his head silently and spooned sugar into his pot of tea. Without even looking up from his Sun newspaper, Stan explained that he would get something in Leeds.

Maureen felt like doing a little dance but managed to maintain her self-control and, instead, put two more pieces of bread into the toaster by means of celebration. 'Getting something in Leeds' meant that Stan would call in at one of the pubs that served Black Sheep — he knew them all — but, more importantly as far as Maureen was concerned, it meant that his palette would, she hoped, already be so suitably fogged by the time she presented him with her 'special' bottle that he might not notice any unusual additional ingredients... or, at least, not until it was too late.

Stan left the house for the ten o'clock Rochdale-to-Halifax bus (he would change for the Leeds bus in Halifax) and Maureen watched him walk along the path with something that might almost — *almost* — have been sadness, short-lived though it was.

The rain started as she finished the washing up, further evidence — if any were needed, she thought — that the gods favoured her plans: the rain meant that any other would-be market gardeners would think twice before spending time in their allotment, so there shouldn't be too many (if any) witnesses to her visit. Even Stan was reluctant to venture out of the house in the rain and, for a moment, Maureen became concerned that the change in the weather might dissuade him from the trip to Leeds.

She sat on the bed watching out of the window until the bus came. She could see the top of it through the gardens across the street though she couldn't see if anyone was standing at the stop. But the bus stopped — so there must have been someone there — and then, just to make sure, she waited a few minutes to see if Stan returned before setting out, her hands encased in a pair of light blue Marigold gloves and the shed key tucked safely in her coat pocket, on the first part of her mission.

By the time she reached Honeydew Lane, the rain had grown heavier and the skies across Luddersedge — and across the entire valley, Maureen reasoned, looking over to the horizon in each direction — were slate grey and menacing.

Maureen slipped through the metal gate, cringing at the sound of hinges in desperate need of a drop or two of oil, and made her way to Stan's section.

She passed the two other neat sections, with rows of trimmed plant-tops (whose identity Maureen neither knew nor cared about) that appeared clone-like in their similarity, and felt a wave of animosity towards them. It seemed as though, as she passed them, they sniggered at her in the wind and she felt like running amongst them, kicking at them with her shoes and swinging with her bag, tearing them out of their loamy houses by a vicious strangulating hold inflicted by her light blue Marigolds. If she had not been so preoccupied with these thoughts of garden-murder, she might have wondered why the three plots across from these three neat ones were so comparatively uncared for.

But she didn't.

As she reached Stan's shed door and inserted the key into the old lock, Maureen felt her pulse quicken. When she was inside, amidst the sudden silence and the smell of creosote and earth, under the accusative eyes of hoes and rakes and spades, she felt even worse: she suddenly realised she needed to go for a 'number two', even though she had already had one that morning. Must be nerves, she thought to herself, scanning the carefully lined-up bottles and cans on the shelf at the back of the shed.

After all, weren't there lots of stories about crooks leaving a mess on the carpet of the homes they burgled? Maureen now had some sympathy for their situation.

She read the various labels, taking care to remind herself mentally every few minutes that under no circumstances must she remove the Marigolds, until she found what she wanted: EXTERMINATE!, an old, tall can whose title appeared on four separate lines — EXT, ERM, IN and ATE!. The label carried numerous warnings printed in bold, red capital letters (DANGER!, CARE! and CAUTION!) and the top around the cap had rusted. Trying to loosen the cap, Maureen doubted that this product was still being made and she hoped (assuming she would eventually get inside) that the contents were still in good working order.

When the top finally succumbed to pressure, Maureen removed it fully and peered inside. There seemed to be plenty there for her purpose and, even better, EXTER-MINATE! had no noticeable smell. Of course, there was always a possibility that Stan was simply using the can to store some other potion — possibly one with few or no harmful effects to humans — but a quick glance across the shelf showed that Stan always used Sellotaped labels denoting the contents when those contents were different to the can containing them.

She replaced the cap, tightly to make sure there could be no leakage into her pocket (even though she intended first wrapping the container in an old Netto's plastic bag) and checked around to make sure there was no evidence of her visit. Once satisfied, she pushed the shed door open slightly and peered out: the coast seemed clear — no doubt thanks to the continued rain — and, without further ado, she slipped out, closed and locked the door, and went on her way... thankful the need for a 'number two' seemed to have gone away.

This time, the plants in the allotment rows did not snigger. This time they were still (though it was probably just that the wind had dropped) and altogether more respectful. "You're all going to die," she whispered into the rain, thinking of the Council letter. "Every one of you."

Once she was safely back on Honeydew Lane Maureen removed the Marigolds and walked down the hill to the Threshers on Eldershot Drive where she bought three bottles of Black Sheep bitter. Then, pleased that she had not seen anyone that she knew (another vote of thanks for the rain!), she made her way back home.

The stage seemed to be pretty well set: now all she needed was the star performer to return from his jaunt.

Maureen's star performer arrived back in the house at a little after four o'clock. Allowing for time spent each way on the bus and an hour or an hour and a half in the pub, he had been in Leeds for more than four hours: you could buy a lot of tools in four hours, Maureen thought. And so wasn't it a little surprising that he arrived back without so much as a single bag? Maybe so. But by this time, Maureen was concerned only with the job in hand.

Thinking ahead, she had realised that leaving the addition of EXTERMINATE! until the actual pouring of the beer itself left room for all kinds of unpleasant developments. Thus, with considerable dexterity, she had opened the bottle — carefully, without bending the cap too much out of shape — poured out a little of the beer and topped it up with the special brew retrieved from Stan's shed. She had considered repeating the exercise with a second bottle (it could only be two at the most because she needed one 'untreated' bottle for another purpose) but felt that one should be enough: anyway, she had ensured a generous dose.

The cap had then been carefully replaced and tapped down with a small claw hammer Stan kept in the bureau drawer in the hall for when Maureen wanted pictures moving around.

Trying to think of all the things she needed to do had caused her head to ache, so Maureen had written them down on one of the sheets of paper by the phone — itemised thus:

* add poison to bottle and replace cap.

* put bottles in pantry (Stan hated his beer to be too cold, so the fridge was out of bounds.)

* give Stan a drink!

(After this particular item, Maureen assumed Stan would be dead although she refrained from any additional note to that effect and opted instead for the exclamation mark.)

* put bottle in dustbin.

* pour out the contents of the spare bottle and leave it by the glass. (Maureen was particularly pleased with this point. Although she stood by her decision to add the poison to the bottle itself and not to the glass, she knew there would have to be a bottle alongside the dead man and she also knew that, although it was hoped that the whole thing would be an open-and-shut case, traces of the poison in the bottle — when the 'victim' had drunk from a glass — would cause unnecessary suspicion.)

* make sure Stan's fingerprints are on the EXTERMINATE (She omitted the exclamation mark on this.) and leave the can beside the bottle and the glass.

* leave the council letter by the bottle, can and glass.

Stan's first port-of-call on arriving home — with little more than a grunted acknowledgement of Maureen's presence — was the toilet. Interrupting the Niagra-like cacophony of his flow as it resounded through the house, Maureen shouted up to see if her husband would like a beer. The answer was an emphatic "Great!" followed by another stream of water (no doubt caused by excitement at the prospect of more beer or the need to make more room for same). The toilet flushed as Maureen took the treated bottle of Black Sheep from the pantry. She was opening it when Stan arrived in the kitchen behind her, an arrival announced by two things: the slurring noise of his feet and Stan's voice saying, "What's this?"

When Maureen turned around, Stan was frowning at her list of things to do... albeit, she was delighted to note, the wrong side.

"It's someone's telepho-"

"Sheila Hilton," Maureen said, springing across the room and doing her best to get the paper back without appearing to snatch it. She stuffed it into her pinny pocket and turned back to the table where Stan's final drink was already half-poured. "I saw Jackie Cartwright the other day at the market in Tod — getting black pudding," she added, filling the lurking silence with unnecessary information that she knew would blank out Stan's concentration (and, more importantly, his curiosity). "And she said she'd call me with Sheila's number. Haven't seen her in years," she added, pouring the final drops from the bottle and squinting down at the now-full glass for any tell-tale signs.

Stan grunted, apparently satisfied with the explanation.

"Do you want a few crisps?" Maureen asked. "Or some nuts?" Considering the imminence of the condemned man's execution, nuts and crisps was as close as she could get to the obligatory 'hearty meal'.

Stan shook his head and plonked himself down at the table.

Maureen watched as he reached for the glass.

Stan looked at her as he raised the glass to his mouth.

Maureen knew that this was the moment beyond which there was no return: if she were to save her husband, now was the time to knock the glass from his hands. But by the time she had thought up an excuse for such a strange action (telling Stan that she had seen a wasp on the rim of the glass seemed like the favourite explanation), Stan had drunk half of the contents. He sat the glass on the table, looked at it for a moment, and then reached for it again, frowning.

"Something up with it?" she asked, hoping he could hear her voice above the drumming thunder of her pulse.

Stan didn't respond. He lifted the glass again and sniffed.

"Is it off?" Maureen enquired, keeping her voice calm.

Stan did one of his usual facial shrugs — a strange lifting of the nose and eyebrows — and put the glass to his mouth. He was halfway through the remaining beer when the glass dropped from his hands and he doubled over on the chair.

Maureen backed away against the cabinet where she kept her best blue-flowered crockery, wincing at the sound of the delicately positioned piles shifting as she hit the cupboard with her bottom.

Stan hit the floor jack-knifed, his big hands anxiously kneading his stomach all the way and even when he was flat out.

The sound that Stan emitted was a long drawn-out groan, but not the kind of sleepy groan he gave when the alarm clock went off (always an alarm clock, even though the only place he ever had to go since leaving the buses was his damned allotment). This groan was the collective sigh of all the souls in hell bemoaning their eternal torment. It was the sound of organs deflating and dying, being seared into immediate submission by a concoction of age-old poison and bottle beer.

"I'll get the doctor," Maureen said, rushing out into the hall, keen to avoid the spectacle of her partner for these past three decades and more melting into the checked and threadbare kitchen linoleum.

She lifted the phone and pretended to hit the buttons, staring at Stan as he writhed around. He called out again a couple of times — words and phrases that Maureen could not recognise — and then he began to howl. Maureen thought about switching on the radio to drown out the noise so that Stan didn't attract attention from the neighbours and then he went quiet. She ran back to the kitchen and knelt down beside him, thinking he might be gone, but when she rested a hand on his shoulder she could feel it shuddering deep down inside her husband's body, as though Stan were a road-digger. "Doctor's on his way, love," she said softly against his ear.

Stan nodded and gave a low whine.

He opened his eyes slowly and the shuddering stopped.

There was a long, drawn-out *phhhht* from Stan's backside and his stare moved slowly until it rested on Maureen's face. She raised her eyebrows, expecting him to say something... to maybe get to his feet and say *Well, nice try old love: now it's my turn!*... stretching his meaty hands out to her throat...

But none of that happened.

What did happen was that Stan's eyes locked on Maureen's and in that split instant she knew that he knew what she had done. Then, without another movement, he went. His eyes were still wide and still in the same position but the life just went from them... fell away from the body like a mist banished by the sun and captured on fast film for one of the nature programmes on the TV.

Maureen got to her feet and thought about doing something about the high-pitched hum she could hear... until she realised that she herself was making it. She clenched her teeth tightly and swallowed.

She got out her piece of paper and read the notes.

The bad bottle went into the peddle bin until she thought better of that and retrieved it to put it into the dustbin outside (along with the light blue Marigolds: a sudden afterthought, just to be on the safe side), beneath all the other stuff they'd thrown away over the past few days.

The contents of a second bottle went down the sink, flushed away by a long run of the cold tap, and the bottle went onto the table. (The third bottle, spared for a while, would languish in the fridge for a few weeks before being consigned, untouched and unused, to the bin long before its sell-by date.)

The letter from the council also went on the table.

She left the glass on the floor.

The poison (duly finger-printed by Stan's limp right hand) went on the table next to the letter.

Then she went and looked out of the windows. Nobody was around.

Maureen went into the hall and phoned the police.

The interview with the police seemed to go well, as far as Maureen could judge these things. She felt she had displayed a suitable mixture of hysteria and disbelief, both of which, she was a little surprised to note, were fairly genuine.

All she kept saying was that she had no idea why her husband should do such a thing... explaining that she had left everything just as she had found it.

She tried to feel unconcerned when one of the officers carefully removed the glass, bottle and EXTERMINATE!, placing them into polythene bags and labelling them.

It seemed to be an open-and-shut case, the detective explained, his voice dripping with regret. Her husband's allotment was his whole life — "No disrespect intended, Mrs. Walker," he had added, to which Maureen had first frowned and then nodded, with a dismissive wave of the hand — and the prospect of losing it had been too much to bear. Stan had brought a can of poison from his shed, mixed it with a glass of beer and... "Bob's your uncle," he said. (Actually, none of Maureen's uncles was called Bob, but she didn't think that that mattered too much.)

The good thing, the detective (a very nice man with a very nice smile, Maureen thought with a slight colouring to her cheeks) assured her, was that Stan wouldn't have suffered... he was sure. He may well have been a nice man with a nice smile, Maureen thought, but he didn't know very much at all about drinking EXTERMINATE!

Would she be all right in the house overnight? (It was now after six o'clock and growing dark outside.) Maureen said that she would and, a little before seven, she was alone. Alone the way she would always be.

That night, she slept soundly.

The next morning, Maureen dressed as sombrely as she felt was appropriate and as frivolously as she felt she dare (considering her 'unhappy' situation).

After a quick breakfast of Alpen and toast — followed by her usual visit to the toilet ("... like clockwork, my bowels," she always delighted in telling Joan Cardew and Miriam Barrett on their communal Monday morning expeditions to the clotheslines) — Maureen left the house early and got the bus to Bradford where she spent the day wandering around the shops and practising how she would respond to all the expressions of condolence she would have to endure.

Where the time went she didn't know.

For lunch, she had egg and chips, bread and butter, two pots of tea and a jam doughnut from a cafe in the market — it was greasy, a little on the tasteless side and the doughnut was rock-hard but, to Maureen Walker (newly-made widow of the parish) it was a banquet fit for a queen... and all for less than two pounds.

More shop-wandering (and practising) in the afternoon and then a visit to the cinema — alone: she felt so *daring!* — to see a film called *Dark City* that she thought might be a thriller but she couldn't understand it: all it seemed to be was a load of buildings growing up out of the ground and then shrinking down into it again, and the ending showed them all out in outer space. Things had come a long way since the likes of Cary Grant and Alan Ladd and, in Maureen's opinion, the trip hadn't been worth the effort.

On the bus going home, Maureen realised that tomorrow she would have to make all the necessary arrangements. Staring out of the windows onto the black countryside, she tried to make a list in her head of how many people she would need to cater for... wondering whether to have a go at making the sandwiches herself or buying them in.

Letting herself into the house, she felt tired and, suddenly, just a little lost. It would pass: it was just the excitement of the past couple of days. She made sure the doors were well locked — going back to them twice to double-check — and made a cup of camomile tea to go to bed with. No sooner had she drained the last dregs, watching her foot stray under the covers into the cool of Stan's side of the bed, than she settled down and drifted off into a deep sleep in which she dreamt of buildings growing up all around her and hemming her in.

The next day, her second morning of freedom, Maureen slept in.

It was after nine o'clock when she was disturbed by a noise downstairs.

She opened her eyes wide and listened.

What had that been? Had it been the stealthy sound of a slippered foot on the stairs... the sound of her husband, returned from the morgue in Halifax General (a journey that had taken Stan a full day and a night to make), slurring along the lonely lanes to Luddersedge to arrive with the-

The postman! That was what it had been.

Maureen got out of bed, slipped into her slippers and pulled on her dressing gown.

On the way downstairs, she could see the single letter on the doormat. Another brown job.

Maureen lifted it up.

Somewhere nearby, a car engine sounded... growing louder.

The letter wasn't even addressed to them but to Luddersedge Development Ltd.... in a swirling, italicised script, at their address for some reason. That disappointed Maureen. Here she was on the first day of the rest of her life and the whole thing had been kicked off with a mistake.

She shuffled the letter inside the envelope until another line appeared above Luddersedge Development Ltd. The line read: *Stanley Walker Esq. Chairman.*

Maureen frowned.

She stretched and turned the envelope over, slitting it open with her finger and removing the single sheet.

As she scanned the letter, she noted that the car engine had stopped. It had stopped somewhere near by.

Maureen read: 'Good to meet you yesterday after so many conversations on the telephone,' the letter began. It was from a firm of solicitors in Park Place, Leeds... someone called K. Broadhurst.

Maureen felt the first indication of a 'number two' approaching — unusual by virtue of the fact that she had not yet had her cereals.

The letter went on to congratulate Stanley and the three fellow members of his (*his! Stanley's?*) consortium on their acquisition of the allotment plots on Honeydew Lane. 'As I pointed out yesterday, the proceeds of the eventual transaction' (K. Broadhurst continued) 'will be considerable' and (he/she was delighted to inform Stan) the purchaser was now prepared to consider 'a high-end six-figure sum but one which was not expected to exceed £800,000'. When payment to the Council had been made — and their own fees deducted, K. Broadhurst seemed keen to point out — the resulting sum should be in the region of £550,000.

Maureen's eyes grew wider and wider as she finished the letter (the signature looked like it might be Kenneth Broadhurst, although the two words were little more than elongated squiggles) and then read it again.

It was The Big One: he had done it. Stanley had brought it off.

When the doorbell rang, Maureen had stopped wondering whether clinching The Big One could ever really be considered a sensible reason to drink a tipple of Black Sheep mixed with EXTERMINATE!

As she made her way to the front door she was worrying that perhaps she should have disposed of the bottle in someone else's dustbin. Or whether any EXTERMINATE! traces had rubbed off on her light-blue Marigolds.

Or even — Maureen thought almost idly, with the need to evacuate the 'number two' now growing perilously urgent as she fast-forwarded all the events of that fateful day — what the police might make of a man who was able to open a can of poison one-handed.

When she opened the door, Maureen was not surprised at all to see that the nice detective wasn't smiling today.

DAVID STUART DAVIES

David Stuart Davies is the editor of SHERLOCK HOLMES - THE DETECTIVE MAGAZINE, and author of several books, both fiction and non-fiction, concerning Sherlock Holmes, including BENDING THE WILLOW, an account of Jeremy Brett's portrayal of Holmes. His latest novel, THE SCROLL OF THE DEAD, was published in May. On the fiction front, he is now examining other avenues away from Baker Street.

David Stuart Davies

INSTANT REMOVALS

Ralph Beaton drove to work in an absent-minded fashion. He had a lot on his mind. His brows corrugated as he contemplated his lot. He was not a happy man. In fact he had not felt at ease with the world, in tune with himself, as it were, ever since that faceless multi-national corporation, International Essentials, had taken over the thriving Leeds firm he worked for. It was not just the fact that he had changed from being a medium-sized cog in a small and friendly machine to functioning as a very small one in a sanitised, impersonal conglomeration, but he also felt, in some strange indefinable way, threatened.

The familiar management had virtually disappeared overnight, pensioned or promoted elsewhere, he assumed; and they had been replaced with an army of tight-lipped, blank-faced, dark suited individuals with nondescript accents. Individuals? Well, no, that was the problem: they were not individuals. In personality, appearance they were as one. His closest colleague, Chris, had left without a word. He had been transferred to one of the overseas branches they had told him, but no forwarding address had been made available for him. And now Ralph felt the pressure for him to go too. Nothing had been said to him directly, but the gaps between the lines were boldly inked in. He just knew they wanted him out. International Essentials wanted their own men.

Ralph pulled up sharply at the roundabout as the furniture van in front of him braked prematurely. The jolt brought his mind back to his journey. Dangerous, that, he thought, losing concentration on a busy road like this.

The furniture van in front of him was open at the back and in the gloom of the interior he glimpsed items of furniture cunningly arranged in a neat and compact fashion: the mainstay and fabric of someone's life on the move. Ralph gave a wry grin. How easily they were collected and whisked away.

As the van pulled forward, a short roll of carpet which had been propped against what looked like an old sideboard, slumped sideways and leant at an awkward angle near the tailboard. It was as Ralph followed the van around the roundabout that he saw the carpet begin to unravel - unravel sufficiently to reveal its remarkable content.

It was a body.

Ralph felt his blood go cold. Surely he was imagining it. His eyes were playing tricks on him. But, no, for as he pulled nearer to the van, staring hard into the dingy interior, he could make out the features of the corpse. It was a middle-aged man, balding, with a dark wound on his forehead. Suddenly the inside of Ralph's mouth grew dry. What on earth was going on? Now, on a straight road again, the furniture van began to surge forward. Automatically Ralph put his foot down on his accelerator. Without thinking it out rationally, he knew he had to follow the van. He had to get to the bottom of this bizarre business, if only to prove to himself that he wasn't going mad.

Mentally he made a note of the number plate.

'RIP 4321. RIP 4321,' he muttered to himself, attempting to commit it to memory.

Despite the speed of Ralph's car, the van was gradually pulling away from him and then, with only the briefest flash of its indicator light, it turned sharp right towards a small leafy side road. Ralph saw the body fall back against the sideboard into its original position, the head lolling in the shadows. An oncoming lorry blared its horn and flashed its lights as the furniture van shot across its path.

As it turned, Ralph caught sight of the firm's name painted in black lettering on the side of the van: Instant Removals. There was no address or telephone number. He waited impatiently, unable to turn right and chase after it because of the continuous stream of traffic barring his way. When at last he was able to move, he roared at great speed down the windy side road, but there was no sign of the van.

'I want to report a murder.'

The expression on the desk sergeant's face did not change. Murder, rape, assassination, you name it, I've had to deal with it, the craggy features and tired eyes told Ralph.

'Oh yes, sir' came the reply after a measured pause.

'Yes, I've seen a dead body.'

'Really.' The tone was laconic, unruffled. Ralph might have easily been reporting a missing dog. 'Where was this, sir?'

'In a furniture removal van.' Ralph was fully aware how ridiculous this sounded.

'In a furniture removal van.' The policeman repeated the phrase slowly, his face immobile, registering no emotion whatsoever.

'Let me explain.'

'That would be useful, sir.' The sergeant leaned forward on the desk cupping his face in his hands and waited for the explanation.

Ralph told him the whole story.

'I see,' said the policeman when Ralph had finished, visibly unimpressed by the account.

'I know how it sounds, but it's the truth. I didn't imagine it,' said Ralph with some passion.

'What's the name and number plate again?'

'Instant Removals. RIP 4321.'

The desk sergeant jotted down the information on a note pad with exquisite slowness, licking the tip of his pencil every few letters. 'Now, sir,' he said at length, 'If you'll just take a seat, I'll see what our computer can dig up for us. I'll just be a little while. There's a coffee machine round the corner, if you'd like a drink. Tastes like dishwater though.' With these words of comfort, he disappeared through the swing doors behind him.

Ralph decided to forgo the coffee and sat on a plastic chair opposite the desk. He looked at his watch and winced. He was already nearly two hours late for work and International Essentials were sticklers for punctuality.

Half an hour went by before the desk sergeant returned. He shook his head sadly before he spoke. 'I'm afraid we can't help you, sir. The information you gave us has drawn a blank.'

'What!'

'There's no trace of a firm by the name of Instant Removals and no vehicle has been registered with that particular registration code. It's a very odd one. Maybe you got it down wrong.'

Ralph shook his head angrily. 'I didn't get it down wrong,' he cried, his voice unnaturally loud.

The policeman narrowed his eyes. 'Are you all right, sir? You seem rather agitated.'

'Of course I'm all right. I'm just concerned that you don't seem to believe me. You think I've imagined the whole thing, don't you?'

'It's not really a case of whether I believe you or not, sir. But ERIC doesn't.'

'Who on earth is ERIC?'

'Our computer: Evidence Research Initiative Computer. He's infallible.'

'So because your computer can't come up with anything on the facts - the facts - I've given you, you're not going to do a thing about it. Is that it?' Ralph's irritation was shifting to full blown anger.

'There's not a lot we can do, sir. Not on the information you provided. We need more details I'm afraid.'

'But a man's been murdered.'

'So you say.'

'What's that supposed to mean?'

'Well, you admitted yourself that at first you thought this "body" was just a roll of carpet. Perhaps...'

'It was a body. I'm certain of it. And the name on the van was Instant Removals. And the registration was RIP 4321.'

The policeman nodded in a well-practised patronising fashion. 'Well, sir, if you'd like to make a statement, we might be able to follow this up at a later date.'

Ralph drove away from the police station in a rage. What a farce, he thought, his hands gripping the steering wheel until his knuckles showed white. Probably they had shoved his statement through the paper shredder as soon as he'd left the building. It was quite obvious that the desk sergeant had thought he'd escaped from somewhere. Bodies in the back of removal vans. Take more water with it next time, eh? Well, it was a fantastic tale he had to admit after his temper subsided. But he was in no doubt about what he had seen. For a fleeting moment the image of the grey-faced corpse flashed into his mind and he winced. He consoled himself with the thought that he had done all he could about it. If the police didn't believe him, it wasn't his fault.

He glanced at the clock on the dashboard. It was just after twelve. The morning was gone. And if the police wouldn't believe him, what chance was there that his new superior at International Essentials would?

He needed a drink. There was quite a nice pub not far from the factory. Ralph decided to call in for a quick pint before facing the music.

Ten minutes later he pulled into the car park of the Fox and Grapes. He was just locking his car when he saw it. The van. The Instant Removals van parked close to the pub's entrance. Without hesitation, he ran over to it and peered into the back. It was empty: no furniture - no body. He looked around him to see if he was being watched but the car park was quiet. No one was about. He checked the number plate and felt a thrill of excitement as he read RIP 4321.

'I knew I was right. I knew I was bloody well right,' he said in a fierce whisper.

Suddenly he heard a noise. A couple of teenage lads tumbled out of the pub, laughing and pushing each other about. With affected nonchalance, Ralph made his way back to his car. Here, he was determined to wait. Eventually the 'removal men' would leave the pub and he would follow them. This time he'd make sure he didn't lose them. He'd get to the bottom of this business, if it was the last thing he did.

After about an hour, two burly characters strolled out of the Fox and Grapes and approached the van. They were dressed in grey nylon overalls with red badges, very similar, Ralph thought, to those worn by the workforce of International Essentials.

When the van drove out of the car park, Ralph was right behind it. As it happened, it moved at a leisurely pace, keeping well within the speed limit.

To Ralph's surprise he found himself tracing the reverse route of his morning journey. As he followed the van up increasingly familiar roads, he felt a gnawing sickness growing in his stomach. It was when the van finally stopped that he froze with horror. They had pulled up directly outside his own house.

Eileen Dewhurst

(Photo: Joan Gray)

Eileen Dewhurst was born and brought up in Liverpool, read English at Oxford, and has earned her living in a variety of ways, including journalism. She has written twenty crime novels: sixteen murder mysteries, three thrillers, and one experimentally combining the two genres. Most recently she has alternated two series: one set in Guernsey and the other featuring actress Phyllida Moon who sleuths in character as a private eye.

Eileen Dewhurst

SEESAW

I*t's Liverpool gentlemen, you know, dear, and Manchester men.*
That was the statement my silly, shallow Aunt Marcia used to trot out at some
stage of my every visit, always with the same pseudo-apologetic little giggle. My
mother thought it had been a catch-phrase circulating the snootier Liverpool suburbs
at the end of the war, but by the time I was old enough to visit Aunt Marcia on my
own it was anything but true: with the decline of the Atlantic shipping trade Liverpool
had lost its cachet and no longer figured among the leading cities of Britain.

Manchester did, though, and still does. A thriving, lively city giving its name to
the country's second airport. My home town. It was because I was a Manchester girl
that Aunt Marcia brought out her catchphrase.

Whenever she did her daughter Elaine would nod approvingly, enjoying an extra
opportunity to feel superior to her Mancunian cousin. I hated those visits to Liverpool
but my mother always insisted I made them. Although we lived comfortably, she
felt that her sister had made a better marriage than she had and wanted me to benefit
from the influence of what she saw as a more elegant lifestyle.

It wasn't that Aunt Marcia and Elaine were unkind to me, apart from that one
little dig. It was just that their self-assurance made me feel even more awkward than
I usually did.

And I *was* awkward. I don't deny it. Awkward and clumsy and very, very shy.
The contrast between my cousin and myself was really painful. I can see us now,
reflected side by side over the years in a succession of cinema, theatre and restaurant
cloakroom mirrors: Elaine's hair falling wavy and graceful and never needing a
comb, mine as I tugged at it sprouting in unbecoming tufts round a face with rosily
shining nose and cheeks however hard I scrubbed them with powder. Elaine had a
creamy matt complexion that never needed any powder at all…

I had one best friend at my grammar school, as shy and gauche as myself. Elaine
belonged to a set of laughing, confident girls at the school where she boarded.
Sometimes I coincided with one or more of them on my visits to Liverpool, and they
seemed to point up my inadequacies simply by being there.

But that was then, and now - I shall never get over the surprise of it - now Elaine
needs me. Needs me morning, noon and night and waits anxiously on my coming…

Elaine's youth continued on its gilded way. In her twenty-first year she made a
very good marriage to a young man already coining it in the City, and went to live in

his Chelsea flat. With the first baby on the way she and Robin moved round the corner to the chic little house where Stephen was born. Two years after Stephen there came Carol. One of each. She even managed that.

I, meanwhile, trained as a nurse in Manchester, and had my fiance walk out on me. He wasn't much cop and I soon got over him, but I didn't get over being celibate - I've a big libido and no sexual bravado, which is a difficult combination. But I threw myself into my work and discovered quite soon that I was an exceptionally good nurse. I worked my way to the top in hospitals, first in Manchester and later in London, and then decided to go freelance. I had excellent references and it was easy to get on the books of a prestigious agency. The work is very well paid.

And now when I look in the mirror (I've just done so) l see a fine figure of a woman, statuesque and high busted, with well-defined features and cleverly cut red-brown hair that falls back into place even in a rain-lashed gale. Though I say it myself I look good in uniform. (Some of my male agency clients have wanted me to pretend not to be a real nurse, but I'm only into the straight and they soon learn how a real nurse can make them regret such impertinence.) So, social confidence at last, as well.

Once I'd left school and could do as I pleased I never visited Aunt Marcia again. Elaine and I, though - I can't think why - continued to exchange Christmas cards. The year I went to London I sent mine early with a change-of-address slip, so that she could send hers to the right place. With it she enclosed a note in her turn, saying that now I was so close we really must meet. Neither of us did anything about it.

And then, ten years or so later, I heard from Robin. By letter, telling me Elaine had had a stroke so severe it had left her unable to move anything but her hands and her head. She could stutter out a few words, and write things down when she wanted to be fluent, and from her comments on books and radio and TV it was clear she could still take them in. But she could do nothing for herself, and although he saw to her needs when he was at home, on weekdays he was at work and there were, of course, other necessities requiring professional help. He knew I was now working as a freelance, and he wondered if there was any chance of my being willing to look after Elaine, taking my place in the family to which I belonged, at least for as long as it took him to find the right long term replacement for the string of unsatisfactory nurses he had been forced to dismiss.

I felt deep shock when I read Robin's letter, remembering that beautiful, quicksilver girl, and I tried not to admit to the sense of satisfaction that came with it, a sort of The Lord giveth and the Lord taketh away feeling that glowed through me as sensually as sexual release. (I always tried not to admit to my frustration at the absence of *that*).

At first I thought that uncomfortable mixed reaction was all Robin's letter had given me, but as I turned it over in my mind during the following few days I discovered that his proposition appealed to me. As he himself had pointed out, I could take the job on a temporary basis, and if it didn't work out I could leave. I had a nice little flat by then in Maida Vale, but if the job suited me I could let it. By the end of the week it seemed absurd not to give the idea a try, and I replied - also by letter - that I would be pleased to talk it over.

This time Robin telephoned me, incoherent with gratitude.

I was shocked all over again when I saw Elaine, my imagination not having prepared me for the transformation of that lovely, lively girl into the gaunt creature slumped in a chair, hair lank and straight, face and figure inert but for the pleading eyes and fluttering hands. By poignant contrast these seemed even more beautiful than I had remembered them, and for a few moments the sense of satisfaction deserted me and there were tears in my eyes. Robin saw them and fervently renewed his pleas, adding that he was, of course, offering full board and an excellent salary.

I accepted. And saw something in Elaine's huge eyes that I couldn't interpret, but which might have been fear. I tried not to feel gratified.

I've been here now for two years, and I still don't know how she feels about having me permanently around. I think often about the contrast between past and present - I'm doing it now - but does she? If she does, it will be far less pleasant for her than it is for me. Whatever, I have no intention of leaving. I had enough of crises, panics, and difficult colleagues in my hospital jobs for one lifetime, and I'm enjoying the peace and security, and the being absolutely in charge.

At first I was wary of the son and the daughter, but I soon realized this was unnecessary. Stephen and Carol simply do not want to know. Stephen has his own place and is already following in his father's Midas footsteps; he finds it difficult now to be with the mother he used to treat like a fun elder sister, and is only too ready to accept my conscience-soothing reassurance that she understands and would hate him to be distressed. Carol is recently married and has settled in Edinburgh. Enough said.

So life is good, and can, I think, only get better.

I had a sad duty, though, this morning: I had to tell Elaine that her husband has cleared out. Bag and baggage. That he's taken everything he owns from the bedroom they used to share (Elaine, now, is confined to the best and largest of the downstairs rooms), and hasn't left a forwarding address.

I was afraid that the shock might carry her off - although it occurred to me at the same time that as she has so little quality of life that could really be for the best. The only clues I have to her state of mind are her hands and her eyes and they went into overdrive, her eyes widening and swivelling and her poor hands beating at the air. If I don't want to feel uncomfortably sorry for Elaine I have to look away from her hands. But this morning, after delivering such devastating news, I took a deep breath, seized one of them in both of mine, and started to stroke it.

I was surprised at the force with which she pulled it away, but I could sense the anger she was unable to express, and I suppose it gave her strength. She shook her head from side to side and kept saying "No," over and over. Eventually she managed "Not. Robin."

I didn't try touching her again but I drew up a chair and sat down beside her. "I think it would be a good idea," l told her, "not to say anything to visitors. And it isn't as though you have so many these days, is it, dear?" That was my long delayed riposte to Liverpool gentlemen and Manchester men and it cleared me of the last of my rancour. "He's all right," I went on "Robin's all right, dear. I rang the office and he was there, they put me on to him. We agreed to tell people for the time being that he's having a bit of a break from the home scene. He said to tell you how sorry he is that he just can't go on any longer and that it would have been too painful to say goodbye. Stephen and Carol know his new address, he said, but they've promised to keep it secret. I suspect he may have had a bit of a brainstorm, and needs absolute peace and quiet. At home, I mean, we both know how restful he finds the office. Perhaps he'll come back, dear, when he's over it. But I don't think we should get too excited. Better a pleasant surprise than a disappointment."

I got up then rather quickly, because she had made a strange sound that I can only describe as a growl. The next minute, though, she was crying, and I handed her my clean handkerchief "Not to worry, dear," l said as she wiped her eyes. "You'll be all right, I'll see to everything. In fact I think we'll do very well on our own."

I don't understand. Robin would never leave me. Robin! The mere idea is absurd. Robin loves me so much he suffers as cruelly as I do whenever we're apart. And Muriel has told me he may have left me for ever! My beloved, my devoted Robin! His presence is all that has sustained me through this terrible nightmare, kept me warm inside this cage which was once my body. Muriel's words have turned that warmth to ice.

And fear. I am terrified. I am writing the word down now on my pad. Terrified. Terrified. Terrified.

Terrified of Muriel. When she told me Robin had left me she stood too close as she so often does, invading my small private space. Does it give her a sense of power over me? She knows I can do nothing about it, that I can't move away from her. And she has a lot of old scores to settle.

I'm terrified of a world without Robin. Robin would never choose to leave me, so I know he can have had no choice. And the only reason he would have no choice is if he was dead.

So he must be dead.

And Muriel must have killed him.

I don't know why Muriel would have wanted to kill Robin, he gave her this job she loves and he never interferes with how she does it. Perhaps it's just that she hates men, I can imagine that. Or because she's mad. I can imagine that, too. That's why she terrifies me.

When Robin offered me a mobile phone I wish I'd accepted it. But I didn't want to hear people hanging up on my stutter. I can ask Muriel to get me one of course, and she'll tell me she'll look into it. But nothing will happen. A mobile phone is the last thing she will want me to have now.

I can talk to a visitor, or Mrs Mop when she cleans my room, beg them to ring the office. But they'll feel they have to speak to Muriel first, and she'll tell them Robin has just gone away for a well-earned break, touching her forehead and looking significant. And then they'll think I'm the mad one and they'll do nothing.

Oh, Robin my darling, where are you? Are you lying at the bottom of the cellar steps, staring sightlessly at your wine bins? Or has she stuffed you pro tem behind the sacks in the toolshed? Knowing Muriel as I now do, I expect she has already neatly and safely disposed of you.

I cannot bear it. I must - I must! - be released from this cage, so that we can be reunited. If I beg Muriel, surely she will oblige? Having killed once she will have few qualms about killing again. My death, anyway, may already be on her agenda. Which would mean that for once we both want the same thing. I hate my cousin the murderess with a deadly hatred, but my release is in her gift, and hers alone. Next time she comes in to me I will petition her.

"Such an idea!" The nurse bridled indignantly, crumpling the offending piece of paper into a ball and shying it successfully at the waste-paper basket. "Asking me to kill you! Saying I'll find it easy because I've done it before! I've never heard such wicked nonsense, Elaine!" Even when she wasn't angry, Muriel tended to speak in short staccato sentences ending with oral exclamation marks. "And accusing me of killing your husband! I told you, Robin has had enough and just felt he must get away. So if you die it won't bring him back to you. And if he's left you in this life he's hardly likely to want to see you in another!" Looking into Elaine's eyes, Muriel saw the pain in them and felt a sudden unfamiliar stab of remorse at having spoken so bluntly. But she had to put the poor woman off such a morbid idea "Well, perhaps

I'm wrong," she conceded. "Perhaps you'll be young and strong again in heaven, and then you *will* come back together." She had been talking half facetiously, but for a moment Elaine's eyes had glowed, and her hands had fallen peacefully together in her lap. Muriel felt another unfamiliar sensation - awareness of another person's feelings - and found herself glad that the look of pain had gone; it had made her feel quite uncomfortable.

But when she got up to the big bedroom her indignation was back in place. Robin was on the two-seater sofa, reading the paper, and she banged down heavily beside him.

"She's just accused me of murdering you, sweetie," she told him. "She probably thinks I've dumped you in the cellar." She suddenly saw the funny side of it and burst out laughing. Muriel's laughter was a back-of-the-gods affair, and Robin clamped his hand across her mouth.

"It's all right," she said, wiping her eyes "She's under the spare room."

"We can't take any risks."

"You worry too much."

"I do worry. Why does she think you killed me?"

"As if you didn't know!" Playfully she pinched his cheek. "She can't believe you'd ever choose to leave her."

She saw him wince, and heard his faint moan.

"Hey! None of that, now!"

"No, no," he assured her, taking hold of her chubby red hand. He would have to forget about Elaine's hands. And her eyes... "It was just... I'm all right. I couldn't have taken another moment." Because he had reached a point where he could no longer bear to look at the remains of his wife. And had been missing for too long a faithful time what Muriel had recently begun to give him...

"That's not all," she was telling him. "She begged me to kill her too so that you could be reunited. Said I would know what to use, that I would have access, and that it would be easy for me because I'd done it before. The cheek of it, sweetie!"

"She has to think you killed me," he said, trying not to shudder as the pang went through him. "I should have realized she was bound to. It's the only way she can explain my disappearance. As it is, she must be desperately unhappy."

"Yes..." Muriel bounced to her feet, her face flaming.

"What is it?"

'There aren't many situations," she answered, slowly sitting down again, "where it's in one's gift to please all parties."

"I don't-"

"She wants to die. We'd be happier without her."

"For God's sake, Muriel-"

"So far as she's concerned, I'm guilty of murder already. And if she ever finds out about you and me - and she will find out, one way or another, eventually - it'll be worse for her than death."

"Yes..."

"It'll be a kindness," Muriel said decisively. "Nobody should live the way she has to. And she's *asked* me, Robin, it's what she wants. She's right about one thing, too, sweetie. I may not have done it before, but I do know what to use and how to get hold of it. There'll be no danger The doctor said she could go any time."

"Oh my God yes." He could not escape her logic.

"I said this set-up would work, and it's working. Trust me again now."

"I will, my Venus." He would never love her, but he adored her self-confidence.

"So why not go down for a bottle of champagne, and we can toast our humanitarian enterprise?"

"But isn't that a bit-"

"It's what we all want, my darling. You, me, and Elaine. That's all you have to think of."

After a kiss that augured well for the later part of the evening, Robin went out on to the landing and tiptoed down the stairs. As he crept past his wife's room he felt better and better, and it was a compassionate and a righteous man who opened his cellar door.

Martin Edwards

(Photo: John Mills Photography)

Martin Edwards has published six novels featuring Harry Devlin who is, like his creator, a Liverpool solicitor. The first, *All The Lonely People*, was shortlisted for the CWA John Creasey Memorial Award for the best first crime novel of 1991. The latest is *The Devil In Disguise*. The books have been optioned for television. Martin Edwards has also published over 20 short stories and edits the CWA's annual anthology as well as the *Northern Blood* series.

Martin Edwards

NEIGHBOURS

9 *July*
This is better than sex.

As a matter of fact, it's *much* better than sex.

I'm beginning to think it may even be better than watching television. And that's saying a great deal, as far as I'm concerned. Perhaps it's a sign that I'm getting choosy. I need something extra, not the same old thing, time after time.

I'm faithful to my favourites, of course I am. *Coronation Street, East Enders, Brookside* and *Emmerdale*. I don't mind the Australian soaps, either. But lately I've had just as much pleasure from the real-life shows. You know, the inside story on life within a hotel, a shopping centre, a driving school. Seeing people who *actually exist* going about their everyday lives. Fly-on-the-wall programmes, they call them, or even docu-soaps. Utterly fascinating, I simply can't tear my eyes away from the screen.

Yet now, it may be - it just may be - that I've stumbled across something that tops the lot.

10 July
They were at it again last night. Talk about hammer and tongs.

He started it. I feel sorry for him, married to her ladyship, but I must admit that he has a dreadful temper. Perhaps it's the forces background - though what happened to military discipline, I ask myself? He's a big man, powerful and the way his voice carries, you'd imagine he was still on the parade ground. At least Philip was gentle. A bit of a bore, maybe, but a gentle bore. Never any violence from him.

Anyway. He'd not been home five minutes when he began to shout at her. I didn't catch the start of it - I'd been on the phone to mum, chatting about the new *Coronation Street* video - but it was all to do with money. Her ladyship's a spender. I see her sometimes, sailing off to the Trafford Centre, plastic cards at the ready. Watching from my front window, I sometimes think that she wears a new outfit every time I see her. Usually with a skirt that barely covers her bottom.

He was ranting about a bill they hadn't paid. She said it was only the gas; they wouldn't be cut off, not with two small children to look after. (Though looking after the little ones doesn't exactly seem to be top of her list of priorities at the moment.) Then she complained that he wasn't earning much from his job. He works at the leisure centre on the other side of the M60. After she said that, things turned nasty.

He said something about the money they owe and then he called her a greedy bitch. She said something about him that was so disgusting I won't even write it down. I was appalled. I wasn't even trying to listen, but the walls in these flats are as thin as tissue paper. When the people next door carry on like that, you simply have no choice but to hear what they are saying. It's terrible, really, that I have to put up with it in my own home. So much for environmental health. What do we pay our council tax for, I wonder?

He went berserk. There's no other word for it. I could hear a thud: he'd obviously socked her one. I could picture the scene just as vividly as if it were on my television screen. Of course, hitting people is wrong, but to my mind she'd asked for it. When she'd got her breath back, she screamed at him, hurled abuse. He slammed the door on his way out, nearly took it off its hinges. Peeping from behind the curtains at the back, I saw him heading for the shed in his garden. He was in there for a few minutes, then he unlocked the gate that gives on to the alleyway behind the flats and disappeared. Probably off to the pub, to drink the evening away. He seems to treat The Eagle and Child as his second home these days. It's a mistake. If he knew what I knew, he'd be sticking close to home. Keeping an eye on things.

Afterwards, I watched *East Enders* and later on, even better, there was the new docu-soap. It's called *Library* and it's all about the characters who work in this big municipal library up in the North East. They're a lively bunch, much more fun than the crowd I work with, thank Heaven. There's a big fat jolly woman who was panicking about an author event she'd organised, and my guess is there's something going on between the girl in the reference section and the publishers' sales rep, the one with the cheeky smile. Tomorrow night, a second series of *Loss Adjusters* begins: the one with the chap who says that his job is to persuade a client who's lost a leg that he's better off hopping. He's a scream. Until I started watching, I'd no idea how interesting that line of work could be. It just shows: you learn so much from television.

11 July

The library closed at lunchtime today, so I was home by a quarter past one. Although it's not a long walk from where I work to the flats, I rushed along as fast as my legs could carry me. The delivery man had promised to call on her this afternoon.

It reminds me of an episode in *Brookside*. A floosy was misbehaving with some chap and her husband came home early one day when they weren't expecting him and he caught them at it. It was a good story, that one. Real human drama. And it proves a point I've often made, especially to Philip when he'd moan that I was always glued to the box. Soaps are just like everyday life. That's why I love them.

His van wasn't anywhere to be seen when I got home. I must admit that I felt disappointed. Cheated, almost, as if he'd personally stood me up. I could hear her next door, pacing up and down. I could tell she was on edge. I made myself a sandwich and a cup of Ovaltine and wondered if he was about to give her the heave-ho. I wouldn't have put it past him. He's not a bad-looking chap if you like that sort of thing, but my guess is that he'll run at the first sign of trouble. She doesn't see that, of course. She thinks he's going to take her away from the flat and her husband. But she has two kiddies at infant school and it's a pound to a penny that lover-boy won't give up his freedom.

At two o'clock, he finally arrived. I heard the van pulling up outside and ran into the living room to have a peek through the window. He looked flustered, not the same as the first time he called here.

I remember that day so well. He was delivering a parcel and he rang my doorbell rather than hers by mistake. I got a good look at him as I pointed out where she lived. He's young, no more than twenty one, at a guess. Five years younger than her - easily.

The flats are in a small two-storey block. One side of this road is lined with them. She and I both live on the ground floor, which is why we have the little gardens at the rear. Our front doors are inches apart. From a distance, though, you might think the place was a pair of semis rather than four flats. When Philip and I split up and I was looking for somewhere of my own, I thought this was the ideal solution. Modern, compact, no need to waste too much time on vacuum cleaning. No stairs to bother with, thank Heaven. What I didn't realise was how shoddily constructed the whole building is.

She chatted him up on the step. I'd left my door ajar - quite by accident - and I could hear every word. Brazen is putting it mildly. She said the parcel was something she was expecting from a mail order catalogue. (She buys a lot of things from catalogues, that's where so much of the money goes.) He asked her to sign for it and while she was writing he told her that he'd had a tough day. He said he'd just started working for this big company with a depot on the outskirts of Warrington and he kept losing his way on the motorway network. Maybe he was just making conversation, more than likely he was looking down the front of that football shirt she likes to wear. A Manchester United replica, it's supposed to be. I gather those things cost a fortune these days. Waste of money, if you ask me.

Anyway, inside a couple of minutes she was telling him that she'd been saving up to buy a new silk nightie. She actually *said* that to a perfect stranger.

Well, one thing led to another. I couldn't believe my ears. Talk about a couple of fast workers. In the end, I couldn't listen to any more. There's only so much that a decent person can take. But I must admit that when he called again a couple of days later, I opened my back bedroom window. Hers was open, too. It's amazing how indiscreet some people are. They have no shame.

It was different this afternoon. I heard him mumble something about running behind schedule and that he couldn't stay long. I wasn't listening to every word - of course, I'm *interested,* but it's none of my business. I'm not a nosey parker. I like to keep myself to myself.

She told him that her old man had hit her. Lover boy sounded nervous. He said she shouldn't put up with it, asked why she didn't call the police or a lawyer, force him to move out. It wasn't what she was hoping to hear, I could tell that right away. She'd wanted him to say that she could move in with him - I can read her like a book. Perhaps she's starting to get worried. She's not a complete fool - it must have dawned on her that he likes the bachelor life. He doesn't want to be caught. I heard her saying something about commitment. He didn't answer. Any idiot could put two and two together, I said to myself.

He went so quiet that I told myself he was having second thoughts. It served her right and yet the funny thing is, I felt so disappointed. Let down, almost. It was as if I didn't want to be deprived of the opportunity to look forward to what might happen next. As if the powers-that-be had decreed that *Coronation Street* had run its course.

She snapped at him. I didn't catch exactly what she said, but the meaning was plain enough. She was telling him to make his mind up. Big mistake. I could have told her myself - men aren't to be relied on. It's a fact. Human nature, call it what you like. It gave him his excuse and within a couple of minutes, he was on his way. Revving up the van as if he never expected to return.

It reminded me of Philip, after he'd told me to choose between him and the telly. I didn't say anything for a while, but I think he came to his own conclusions. His face was as red as a beetroot as he rushed out of the living room. Well, it wasn't my fault. He did ask.

12 July

This afternoon, her ladyship and I had words. It began as something and nothing, really, she was upset because I'd shoved her wheelie-bin out of the way when I was late setting off for work in the morning. It was blocking my path and when the bin men didn't empty it, she hit the roof. She made some very hurtful remarks. Extremely personal. Needless to say, her language was choice. I think they used to talk about fishwives swearing. Believe me, her ladyship would make the average fishwife sound like Barbara Cartland.

I could have retaliated, told her that she was as common as muck, that I knew precisely what dirty tricks she got up to with her delivery man. But I held my tongue.

All the same, I couldn't stop thinking about it, brooding over what she said until this evening. Then I was able to take my mind off things. Two soaps, *Children's Hospital* and a new series about vets. Bliss. Thank Heaven for the wonders of technology, and in particular the video recorder. And yet - I realise now that even the best soaps aren't quite as good as the real thing.

13 July

Lover boy came round this afternoon while her husband was at Old Trafford, watching the match. It was kiss and make up time. He's like a moth to the flame, he simply can't resist her. He doesn't seem to see that it can never work. They aren't meant for each other. I could have told him. It's an old, old story. I've seen it played out in a thousand half-hour episodes.

He cut it fine, too. He stayed much longer than usual. In the end, they must have panicked. I saw him running down the path to his van, tucking his shirt flap into his trousers. Just as well he made his getaway when he did. Not five minutes later her husband was parking his old banger outside the front door. He slammed the car door shut as he got out. You didn't have to be Sherlock Holmes to work out that United had lost.

I hate football, loathe it, but I couldn't help feeling sorry for him, even when he started shouting at her whilst I was trying to watch *Casualty*. She's treating him like dirt.

14 July

Sunday. The worst day of the week so far as the box is concerned. Is it any wonder that I finished up in the bedroom, listening to what was going on next door?

The truth is, I'm hooked. We're barely acquainted, yet I know the most intimate details of their lives. It's sad, but it's fascinating. Of course, it'll all end in tears. It always does. But *how*? That's the question.

She was in a bad temper, maybe withdrawal symptoms because she'd not been able to see her fancy man. At one point, she even cracked a joke about Viagra. I won't repeat it, it's not the sort of thing I'd like to see put down in black and white. I must admit, I thought that she'd gone too far. But he didn't seem to react. Just took himself off to the other bedroom and locked the door. Her ladyship wasn't bothered. She's looking forward to tomorrow, I'll be bound.

And to tell the truth, so am I.

15 July

I called in sick today. I know it was wrong, but I did have a bit of a headache and besides, I wanted to follow the latest instalment of the goings-on next door. Honestly, it's riveting.

Her husband was out early. She was still in bed when he left, the lazy cow. I don't think they even uttered one single word to each other. She was up and doing by the time the van arrived, though. Oh yes. She flung the door open even as he had his finger on the bell. I was in the front room at the time and I managed to catch a glimpse of her. She was wearing a housecoat. From what I heard after they went inside, she hadn't bothered to put on anything underneath it. A slut, you see. She deserves what's coming to her.

After they'd been in bed five minutes, I'd heard enough. More than enough. I mean, how dare she? She turns my stomach and that's a fact. Decent folk can only take so much. I looked up the phone number of the leisure centre. Before I knew what was happening, he was on the other end of the line.

'You'd better get home and get home fast,' I said.

'What is this?' He sounded angry, bewildered. Who wouldn't be, in his shoes?

'Never you mind.'

'Is that you, Mrs Irlam?'

My knees almost buckled when he spoke my name. I thought I'd been rather clever in disguising my voice. I'd tried a faint Irish accent. But he'd seen through my little ruse. Of course, I panicked. Anyone would.

'You need to see what your wife gets up to when you're out of the way,' I gabbled.

I put the phone down before he could ask any more questions and sank back into my chair. I was panting. My nerves were at full stretch. But I was excited, too.

Later

I wrote up my diary while I was waiting for him to come home. I couldn't concentrate on anything else. But I never guessed what he was going to do.

I still had my pen and this diary in my hand when I heard the old banger pull up outside, followed by his footsteps as he crossed the patch of grass which divides the flats from the road. He headed round the side of the building and into the garden. I ran to the back room and caught sight of him peering into the window of his own bedroom. His face was a picture, but he didn't utter a sound.

Instead, he trembled a little, as if making up his mind. Then he hurried off to the garden shed and hid himself inside.

I was puzzled. What on earth was he doing in there? When the shed door opened again, I had my answer.

He'd dressed himself from head to toe in combat gear. A gun of some kind was slung over his shoulder. I couldn't believe my eyes. It was like something on the telly.

I ducked my head down so that he couldn't see me. I was thrilled - who wouldn't be, with a drama on their own doorstep? - but I was frightened too.

And then it occurred to me. It was *exactly* like the telly. *It was as if I'd written the script of an episode for my favourite soap.*

I fumbled for the diary and my pen. I'd brought them with me into the bedroom. I started to write.

Later

Oh God, oh God, oh God. This is a nightmare.

I heard a scream next door. Like a wild animal, caught in a trap. Her ladyship.

Then there were two muffled bangs. After that, nothing.

I have a phone on my bedside table, but when I picked it up, the line was dead. He's thought of everything.

I know my scrawl is barely readable now, but I need to make a record. I'm not writing the script any more. I'm living it.

I need to escape. Outside there is still this dreadful silence. Perhaps he's gone. He must have, surely.

I can't stay here on the floor for ever. This is what I'll do. I'll risk it. I'll get up slowly and very carefully, then look through the window to see if the coast is clear.

Now for it. I can't hear anything. It must be safe, thank

Ron Ellis

Ron Ellis is the author of a series of crime novels published by Headline featuring the Liverpool DJ/Private Eye, Johnny Ace.

In his time he has been a Librarian, Entertainment Agent, DJ, Journalist, Landlord, Salesman, Creative Writing Lecturer, Teashop Proprietor, Actor and Promotions Manager for Warner Brothers Records.

Ron lives on Merseyside with his wife and two teenage daughters. He broadcasts regularly on local radio, covers Southport FC matches for the press and owns a property company in London's Docklands.

A Black Comedy by Ron Ellis

BEHIND THE WHEEL

The cat was called David, a good Jewish name, well suited to an animal of his magnificence. He was a white Persian, a large cat with long matching whiskers, an impressive bushy tail and a pleasing disposition.

He belonged to Wendy Goldman, an attractive girl in her late twenties who had once been married to an upwardly mobile executive in the oil industry but who was now, sadly, a widow.

Bernie Goldman had been a health fanatic. Throughout his life, he'd eschewed all alcohol, never smoked and had been an obsessive vegetarian.

A firm believer in the benefits of regular exercise, he'd installed a fully fitted gym in the cellar of their detached mansion in Southport and always took a swim in the heated outdoor pool after his daily workout.

He boasted several athletic achievements. He once finished 789th in the Manchester Marathon, had a seven handicap at golf and won the men's singles at the Birkdale Tennis Club three years running.

It was during the previous summer, on one of his early morning keep-fit runs, that he collapsed with a fatal heart attack. He was just twenty-eight.

"So much for Charles Atlas chest expanders and low calorie yoghurt," complained Wendy to friends who tried to comfort her after the funeral. "He might just as well have smoked fifty Full Strength a day like his father."

"But he would still have died even then," the friends pointed out, as they digested the post-burial sandwiches. "Wasn't it a defective valve?"

"Yes," conceded Wendy, "although that makes him sound like a wireless."

The Goldmans had not been blessed with issue so, after Bernie's demise, Wendy lived on alone in the five-bedroom house beside Hesketh Park, with only David for company. Not being ready for a new relationship, she invested most of her emotional commitment in her cat.

On this particular Spring day, David was sunning himself outside his home, permitting neighbours and casual passers-by to admire him as he stretched out conspicuously in the middle of the tree-lined road.

Unfortunately, despite his immense size and dazzling white fur, he was not quite conspicuous enough to gain the attention of the elderly driver of a 1985 harvest gold Metro, a matriarchal old lady called Mrs. Partington.

It was debatable whether Mrs. Partington should have been allowed behind the wheel of a car at all. She was seventy nine and a half, deaf in two ears, suffered from failing eyesight and was given to the odd helping of medicinal sherry. A bottle at a time.

She wasn't driving particularly fast but she was discussing an important tactical manoeuvre with her contract bridge partner on her mobile phone and didn't notice David lying in front of her.

David, in turn, was fast asleep and dreaming of his regular evening treat of pilchards in aspic when the Metro hit him.

The tyres came into contact with his paws at twenty-nine miles an hour.

Mrs. Partington felt the bump which was followed by an anguished howl of such intensity that it pierced even her drink-sodden brain. She managed to stop the car by the simple expedient of braking without engaging the clutch, stalling the engine and sliding untidily into the gutter a few yards down the road.

Alerted by the howl, passers-by raced to the scene, including Wendy Goldman who had been sunbathing in her front garden. She examined David who lay still on the ground, his front legs hanging at an unusual angle, then ran over to the Metro.

Mrs. Partington was slumped over the steering wheel muttering angrily to herself, annoyed she might be late for her afternoon of cards.

With great presence of mind, Wendy opened the driver's door of the Metro and removed the keys from the ignition. "Wait there," she instructed the bemused old woman and she rushed indoors to phone the police. She was determined the driver would not go unpunished.

After a three-minute wait, her 999 call was answered. "There's been a road accident," she cried, "in Belvedere Road."

"Is anyone injured? Is an ambulance required?"

Wendy thought quickly. If she told them that only a cat had been hurt, they might not be so keen to come. Cats, like hedgehogs and water voles, were unreportable animals so policemen attending the accident would be unlikely to gain any promotion points. Not unnaturally, therefore, officers of the law were little inclined to race to feline accidents.

She adopted a high-pitched wail. "It's my David. He's been run over outside my house. He was only crossing the road. Please hurry." She emitted another wail. "I think the driver's been drinking."

That should get them here quickly, she thought, slamming the receiver down. She went on to phone the vet and urged him likewise to hurry down forthwith.

The vet arrived first and announced that David had sustained two broken legs and was suffering from concussion but his condition was not life threatening. He took him back to the surgery to operate on the injured limbs which, he assured Wendy, would be 'as good as new in no time'.

The police arrived some ten minutes later, two young constables in a Panda car. One looked too young to shave whilst his partner was white and wore wire-rimmed spectacles.

At first they were not amused to learn that David was a Persian cat but Wendy Goldman did look fetching in her minuscule bikini and, after all, they did have a possible drunken driver to arrest.

"Blow into this," the first young constable barked at Mrs. Partington who was still in her seat, having somehow tied herself up in her safety belt in an ill-judged attempt to flee the vehicle.

With shaking hands, she took the plastic bag to her lips, exhaled fiercely and watched in confused fascination as the contents turned a bright green.

"Bloody cat," she grumbled as she was charged. She cursed her ill luck and wished she'd never stopped.

Her family was not impressed.

"But it's so annoying," she complained to her daughter, Julia. "The beast wasn't even killed for God's sake. I only crushed a couple of its legs."

"It only had four to begin with," pointed out Julia. "Maybe if it had been a centipede it might not have mattered so much. A centipede would have had another ninety six to keep it moving, as it were." She looked her mother in the eye. "It was about time they banned you. You're not fit to be on the roads. You're like a mobile distillery."

"It's the only pleasure I've got left since your father died."

"Drinking or driving?"

"Both."

"Well at least you won't be able to do them together any more."

She was wrong. Three weeks later, Mrs. Partington was back behind the wheel.

Well, the old lady told herself, it was raining pretty hard and the next bus wasn't due for at least an hour. She was already late for the bridge club and the rubber couldn't begin without her so she would be keeping them all waiting.

Thus was she able to justify taking the car. She had, of course, had a couple of sherries. Or was it three? Anyway, it was only two miles down the road. Nobody would know.

The accident was entirely the child's fault. Nobody ever disputed that. It simply lost control of its skateboard. End of story.

It was just unfortunate that it was cruising down the slight incline of a road adjacent to the main road at the very moment Mrs. Partington was approaching in her Metro.

In an ideal world, the child would have stopped its skateboard at the corner but, instead, it hurtled into the path of the alcoholic septuagenarian who had no chance of avoiding it.

With the sudden clarity that six sherries brings to the mind (they were doubles), Mrs. Partington sized up the situation in a second. The road was deserted. Nobody had seen her. She remembered the trouble that ensued when she ran over the stupid cat.

She drove on.

But Mrs. Partington was mistaken. Somebody had seen her. Her daughter, Julia, had heard her start up the car and had immediately jumped into her own car and followed her, with the intention of bringing her back.

She was too late. It was Julia who pulled up beside the immobile skateboarder and summoned the ambulance from her mobile phone as her mother disappeared into the distance.

The ambulance was of little help. "It's manslaughter," declared the police traffic patrolman who was next on the scene.

Julia knew it would be just a matter of time before her mother was caught. Forensic didn't miss things like paint on skateboards and human skin on car bonnets.

Furthermore, the child turned out to be the son of a local councillor. All stops would be pulled out to trace the driver and Julia knew that nothing was going to keep her mother out of jail this time.

Julia was getting tired of her mother's bad habits. Since the old lady had come to live with them, her presence had caused considerable discontent between her husband, Leonard, and herself. Julia feared that if things continued as they were, Leonard might leave her.

Now, more trouble faced them. The nearest prison was fifty miles away. How would Leonard take to a regular weekend round trip of a hundred miles?

More to the point, how would Mrs. Partington stand up to the rigours of a woman's prison? Julia had heard dreadful stories about such places.

Julia decided she would be doing the old lady a kindness by putting her to sleep.

She confided in her husband. "I don't want you to think I'm doing this for the money, Leonard. The £350,000 we would inherit isn't a factor here. No, I just think it would be the best thing for her. There won't be any bridge parties in cell block whatever and she'll miss her regular daily tipple."

Hourly tipple, thought Leonard. "If you think so, my dear." Leonard was used to agreeing with his wife whom he had come to realise was a younger version of her mother. In fact, Leonard wished the two of them could be incarcerated together and leave him to get on with his life in peace.

"Oh yes I do." She became quite enthusiastic. "I'll buy some poison from the drug-store first thing in the morning."

After due consideration, Julia changed her mind about the poison and settled for sleeping pills which she got from her mother's own doctor. "The poor dear's been having nightmares since she ran over that poor cat," she explained.

"These will help her," the doctor reassured her. "They're extra strong. Make sure she only takes one at a time."

"We won't use them yet," Julia told Leonard when she returned home. "We must wait until just before the case comes up. That will provide the reason for people to believe she killed herself."

The Law duly caught up with Mrs. Partington, helped by an anonymous telephone call from Julia informing them of the registration number of a gold Metro she'd seen speeding away from the accident.

"I'm afraid it's looking bleak," Mrs. Partington's family solicitor informed her. "Manslaughter, driving whilst banned and without insurance. I believe you had a bald tyre as well. Luckily, they apprehended you too late for the breathalyser otherwise your sentence could have been even longer. As it is, I fear you look like spending your eightieth birthday as a guest of Her Majesty."

Privately, he thought the old crone would be lucky to be out for her eighty-fifth but discretion prevented him from saying so.

A week before her mother's court appearance, Julia decided to carry out her plan.

"I'll slip half a dozen of them into her evening cup of Ovaltine," she told Leonard. "She won't notice any difference in taste, not with the amount of whisky she puts in it."

"What about a suicide note?" suggested Leonard. "It won't be hard for you to copy your mother's spidery handwriting."

"Good idea." Julia went to fetch a writing pad and pen. "What should I put?"

"Let's see. How about 'Can't face the disgrace. The family name has been ruined. Sorry to leave you this way'"?

Julia scribbled the words down as Leonard spoke them. He read over her shoulder. "Yes, that seems all right." He took it from her.

"Hang on, I've got to sign it yet."

"No need," said Leonard firmly. "They'll know who it's from. We'll put it beside the body."

Leonard spent the evening at a meeting of the Origami Society held at Birkdale Library. Julia watched television with her mother.

At ten o'clock, Mrs. Partington rose from her chair and announced she would make their evening drink.

Julia followed her mother into the kitchen and watched as she boiled the milk and poured it into two matching mugs. As the old lady reached up to the top shelf of the pine kitchen unit for the Ovaltine, Julia seized her chance.

She took the bottle of sleeping tablets from her pocket and slipped six capsules into the left mug, making sure her mother had her back to her all the time.

She forgot about the kitchen mirror.

Mrs. Partington happened to glance across to it at the very moment the small white tablets were descending into her mug. She said nothing.

Julia was probably giving her something to help her to sleep but she didn't agree with all these modern drugs. Besides, if she overslept, she'd have to make her own breakfast. But she wasn't going to argue with her daughter who had a sharp tongue at the best of times.

She carefully measured two tablespoons of Ovaltine into each cup and stirred them both in turn.

"I think that's the doorbell, dear," she said. "I wonder who it can be at this time of night?"

"I didn't hear it," said Julia, puzzled, but she went to look anyway. The second she was out of the door, Mrs. Partington quickly swapped the cups around then added a generous measure of Glenfiddich to what had once been the cup on the right.

She was so busy doing this that she failed to notice Leonard appear through the back door. But he had seen her swap the mugs around.

"I've brought you an individual custard tart from Tesco's, Mother," he smiled, holding up a paper bag. "Get yourself a plate."

Mrs. Partington did as she was bid but Leonard's hand slipped as he opened the bag, causing the tart to slide out and land under the table.

"Look what you've done," she barked, shoving him to one side. "Keep out of the way, I'll get it." She couldn't stand her son-in-law fussing around her. His halitosis and the traces of breakfast Shredded Wheat in his beard made him unpleasant to be close to.

She bent down to retrieve the fallen confection but Leonard caught her hip with his knee, causing her to lose her balance and tumble clumsily to the floor.

Because she was lying with her nose in the splattered tart, Mrs. Partington failed to notice Leonard slip a handful of tablets into her new mug, tablets strangely similar to Julia's.

"There's nobody there. Good God, what's going on?" Julia returned to the room to see her mother on all fours, her face dripping with custard.

"Nothing to worry about, dear." Julia was immediately suspicious. Leonard sounded almost chirpy, not his usual morose self. "Just a little accident. All cleared up now."

"Mmmm." Julia helped her mother to her feet and remembered what she was in the middle of doing. She would have a word with Leonard after her mother was dead.

She carried the two mugs into the living room and sat on the sofa, her mother beside her.

"Drink up, Mother," she said, "before it gets cold," carefully passing her the erstwhile right hand mug. Julia picked up the other mug and they drank simultaneously.

Leonard watched with interest from the doorway. His mother-in-law expired first, probably due to the alcohol in her blood stream, which would have accelerated the effects of the two grams of Nembutal.

Julia's end occurred just a few minutes later. One choking grunt from that familiar accusing mouth and she was gone.

Leonard thought it had been a good idea of his wife's about the Ovaltine. But it had been an even better one of his to include Julia in the plan too.

He'd even got her to write the joint suicide note, being careful to dictate it without pronouns so that it would serve as a joint declaration of both mother and daughter's intention to die. Make the coroner's job easier.

He'd done Julia a favour really. She would only have suffered terrible guilt and remorse when she realised the enormity of her crime. He'd saved her from that.

He would wait until morning to ring the police. Tell them he'd had an early night and found them both when he came down to breakfast. He must remember to cry.

He wondered how long it would be before he received his £350,000 inheritance, not that that had been a factor in his plans, of course.

Once the funerals were over and the fuss had died down, he would maybe go and see that nice young widow down the road, Mrs. Goldman.

He'd heard all about her from Julia after his mother-in-law had run over her cat. During this last week, he'd even strolled past her house a couple of times and seen her in the garden wearing an extremely brief bikini. He'd seen the cat too, a great white hairy thing with bandages over its front paws.

Leonard thought it would be a nice gesture to go round and inquire after the animal's health. Mrs. Goldman...Wendy... would be touched by his solicitude, especially in view of his own recent distressing loss.

He might even take along some fresh prawns. Most cats liked prawns. What was it called again? Something odd. That was it. David.

David! What a ridiculous name for a cat.

REGINALD HILL

(Photo: Rosemary Herbert)

Reginald Hill was brought up in Cumbria where he has returned after many years in Yorkshire, the setting for his award-winning crime novels featuring Andy Dalziel and Peter Pascoe; their investigations have been successfully brought to the small screen by BBC Television. His latest series detective is the redundant lathe operator turned private eye, Joe Sixsmith. In 1995, Reg Hill was awarded the CWA Diamond Dagger and last year won the Short Story Dagger for "On The Psychiatrist's Couch".

Reginald Hill

THE THAW

The snows which had fallen so heavily at Christmas were still there in March. Twice the temperature rose and the streams off the fellside began to swell, and twice Carpenter had laid out his gear in readiness. But each time the wind had turned back into the North and West, whipping old snow and new into another savage blizzard.

The second of these came early in March and set the local farmers complaining loudly of huge lamb losses. Carpenter listened to them in the village pub, nodding in sympathy and noting every word of local weather lore. He said little himself but kept up a front of conviviality, partly for the sake of his fellow drinkers but partly also because the very effort of pretence helped stave off the depression which could grip him as numbingly as the nightly frost gripped the snow-pleated hills.

For their part the farmers were used to his presence now, as one gets used to a crowned tooth, hardly giving it a thought yet still aware somehow of its strangeness.

Their greeting this night was the same as always, guardedly welcoming.

'Evening, Mr Carpenter. What fettle?'

'Fine, fine,' said Carpenter, warming his hands at the fire and stamping his feet.

'You chose a bad winter to stay on.'

'Ay,' interjected George Thwaite, who had sold Carpenter the tumbledown cottage on the eastern boundary of his land four years earlier and glumly watched prices rise ever since. 'You'd have done best to go home after Christmas.'

His tone was light, but the chorus of assent which went up round the bar had a knowledgeable ring, as though the assembled drinkers were in no doubt whose fault it was that the winter had been so hard.

Carpenter walked the three miles to the pub almost every night, except Wednesday. Wednesday nights, he sat and waited for Mary to telephone. At first the calls had been more frequent, gone on longer. Night after night Carpenter had found himself repeating the same assurances that it would soon be over and that it was best that he remained alone in the cottage, till finally constant use bleached all colour and texture out of the words. But by then the calls were down to one a week and soon there was as much silence as conversation. After replacing the receiver, Carpenter would sit perfectly still for a while, trying to conjure up a picture of Mary. But at best all he got was a vague shadowy outline which soon faded away into a white vacancy like driven snow.

There were other calls. His agent rang occasionally to ask how the work was going. He had thoroughly approved Carpenter's sudden decision not to return to London after Christmas but to stay in Cumberland and finish his new book. But now he was faintly suspicious.

He had cause to be. Carpenter hadn't written a word for over two months.

Friends rang from time to time, asking when he was returning to London and filling him in on all the current gossip. He heard several versions of the split-up between Mary and Jack, all full of circumstantial detail. It should have pleased him but it took all his time to pretend surprise and interest. Some of the callers fished for week-end invitations, formerly very plentiful. Carpenter pleaded pressure of work but he was always conscious that he was acting out of character, though soon he began to find it almost as hard to remember his 'normal' behaviour patterns as to recreate an image of Mary. The old Carpenter seemed like a childhood friend, once close, but now through time and circumstances drifted almost beyond recall.

He glanced at the pub clock. The 'new' Carpenter usually left around nine, and it was a quarter past already. The lonely cottage three miles up the valley seemed even less attractive than usual, but he did not feel part of the circle of noisy merriment round the huge open fire. He finished his drink, said good-night, and left.

He had only gone a few hundred yards up the dark narrow road when the roar of an engine fragmented the deep snow-silence and he saw his shadow cast before him by headlights. He stood aside and the vehicle came to a halt beside him.

It was the police mini-van which Dave Wilkinson, the local sergeant, drove. He had met Wilkinson a couple of times and quite liked him. They shared a common 'foreignness' as the sergeant came from the distant shores of Cheshire. More important, he had an open and informed mind and was good company in a conversation on matters other than lambing and the cost of silage.

'Like a lift?' called Wilkinson.

'Thanks,' said Carpenter, climbing in.

'Grand night,' said Wilkinson as the van moved forward. 'I don't think the frost's as hard.'

'No,' said Carpenter, his eyes watching the dark line of road unfurl before them. Its surface had been cleared of snow and the frost lay on it like a reflection of the stars in the hard black sky. On either side rose ramparts of snow-sweepings, higher than the hedgerow in places; and in the fields the smooth expanse of white picked out by the headlights sent the eye racing forwards, seeking a break, till suddenly the fields were behind and the moonlit fells crowded the sky, their equal whiteness broken only by the sheer outcrops of rock where no snow could cling.

'I wanted a word with you,' said Wilkinson. 'I meant to call earlier, but there was a bit of a panic. The Mountain Rescue was alerted. Some kids were late coming back. You'd think people'd have more sense than to let them loose on the fells in this.'

'No trouble, I hope,' said Carpenter.

'No. They landed back at the hostel all right; I had a good talk with the man in charge,' he added grimly.

The road surface got more slippery as they climbed up the valley and the sergeant concentrated on his driving till the mini-van had bumped up the frozen-rutted lonning which led to Carpenter's cottage.

'Come on in,' said Carpenter.

'You've got it nice,' said Wilkinson looking round the cosy living-room.

On a table in a corner, the phone began to ring, an alien startling noise in the snow-silence which seemed to have penetrated even here.

Carpenter started stirring the dormant fire, willing the noise to stop.

'I'll do that,' said Wilkinson, taking the poker. 'You take your call.'

Turning his back on the policeman, Carpenter lifted the receiver and pressed it tight to his ear. He had no doubt who it was and it must mean trouble.

'Carpenter here,' he said.

'Where've you been? I've been trying to get you all night.' She sounded hysterically querulous.

'I'm just back from the pub,' he said lightly. 'You're lucky to find me in now. I would have still been on the road if I hadn't got a lift.'

There was a pause.

'Is there still someone with you?'

'That's right.'

'Some strapping peasant lass airing her big red bum on the hearth-rug, I suppose?'

'Nothing like that.'

'No matter. You enjoy yourself while you can. The police have started asking questions.'

'Is that so? Nothing serious, I hope.'

'Serious? Of course it's serious!'

'I shouldn't worry,' said Carpenter soothingly. 'It's only what we expected.'

'That's fine for you! All you have to do is hang around up there enjoying yourself. But I think you ought to know that your name came up. So just think about that while you're sampling your rustic bloody pleasures!'

The phone was slammed down viciously.

'Bye,' said Carpenter gently and replaced his receiver.

'Bloody nuisance, phones,' said Wilkinson. 'There now, I've fixed the fire. We'll soon be warm. Outside at least.'

He straightened up and stirred the burgeoning fire with his boot.

'There's some scotch on the dresser,' said Carpenter. 'Help yourself. And tell me what this is all about.'

He sat down by the fire and stared into the flames. Talking to Mary had dulled his mind when it needed to be at its most alert. Even her voice seemed changed and foreign now.

'It's about a Mr John Yates,' said Wilkinson. 'I believe he was staying with you at Christmas ?'

'That's right. And Mary, Mrs Yates. Nothing's the matter, I hope?'

It was surprisingly difficult to act out one's own estimated reactions, Carpenter had discovered. His words sounded stilted, unmistakably false, like the opening lines in an amateur play spoken by someone you know intimately.

'Have you heard from Mr Yates since you last saw him ?'

'Why yes. He rang me to say they'd reached home safely. And I got a ... no, I'm sorry. It was Mary who wrote it. They sent me a thank-you note, but it was Mrs Yates who wrote it.'

'So you haven't heard from or seen Mr Yates since, when was it, sir ?'

'Let me see; they left on the twenty-eighth, I think. Two days after Boxing Day, that was it. No, I haven't heard from Jack since he rang that night.'

'And Mrs Yates?'

'Well, no. Apart from the thank-you letter, only indirectly.'

'Could I ask you what you heard indirectly?'

Carpenter hesitated, only half-acting now. He was remembering that this sergeant was a lot more astute than a rustic policeman had a right to be.

'I heard from mutual friends that Mr and Mrs Yates had split up. Or to be more precise, that Jack had packed his bags and left. I wrote to Mary saying how sorry I was to hear this.'

'I see. You wrote to Mrs Yates, you say?'

'Yes.'

'You didn't write to Mr Yates as well?'

'Well no,' said Carpenter, slightly taken aback. 'I didn't know where he was, did I? But I heard that Mary was still living in their old home.'

'Otherwise you might have written to him?' persisted Wilkinson.

'Yes, of course. I don't see ...'

'I was just trying to establish which of the two, Mr and Mrs Yates, was your point of contact, sir. Normally with a married couple, a man knows the husband best.'

'In this case, there was absolute parity of affection,' insisted Carpenter, wondering whether he ought to show offence at the possible overtones of Wilkinson's last comment. 'I was deeply distressed to hear they had separated.'

'But not distressed that Mr Yates seemed to disappear completely thereafter?'

Now Carpenter felt able to let himself go.

'For God's sake what do you mean, disappeared? As far as I was concerned, I just hadn't heard from him for a few weeks. Sometimes months, as much as a whole year could pass without my hearing from him, and that's with us both living in London.'

Wilkinson seemed quite unperturbed by Carpenter's small outburst.

'Yes, your permanent address is London, isn't it? But this year you decided to stay on here after Christmas?'

'That's right. I've told you before. I wanted some peace and quiet to finish a book.'

'You picked the right place,' commented Wilkinson, carefully pocketing the small pad on which he had been making notes. He looked approvingly round the room.

'You've got it nice,' he said again, rather sadly. He now looked ready to leave. Carpenter felt relieved but also felt that something more would be expected of him.

'What's this all about, Sergeant? I don't want to distress Mrs Yates by ringing her to find out. Do you really believe something's happened to Jack?'

'All I know, sir,' said Wilkinson from the door, 'is that early in the New Year, Mr Yates left his wife. No one has seen him since.'

'He does move around a lot. He's a free-lance photographer,' offered Carpenter.

'I gather so. That's probably why it's taken so long for his absence to be noted. In the end it was some of his business associates who started getting worried when he didn't make contact. Evidently he'd made arrangements for money to be paid to his wife, so she just assumed he was keeping out of her way for personal reasons.'

'I hope to God he's all right,' said Carpenter fervently.

They stood together outside the cottage, staring, as one always did in these parts, up at the heights. A stiff breeze had started up from somewhere, blowing across the snow-smooth slopes, drawing plumes of white into the black sky.

'They got on O.K. when they were here, did they?' asked Wilkinson casually.

'Why, yes. I think so. The usual marital friction, but no sign of anything deeper.'

'You're not married, Mr Carpenter?'

'No. Why?'

'It was just what you said. The *usual* marital friction.'

'I'm a writer, I observe things,' said Carpenter drily. 'Lots of married friends take pity on me for meals and week-ends, so I'm quite expert. I try to return hospitality by inviting them here. Like the Yateses at Christmas.'

'Of course, sir. Very nice too. But no one since then.'

It was a statement, not a question.

'I've been busy.'

'Well, I'll keep you no longer. If you do see or hear from Mr Yates, would you mind letting us know? Once we know he's alive and well, our interest ends of course. Goodbye, Mr Carpenter.'

He climbed into his van, wound down the window after starting the engine, and stared expertly into the sky.

'I wouldn't be surprised if we see a thaw soon,' he said. 'Cheerio.'

The thaw began two days later. Suddenly in the valley everything was wet. Water dribbled off the roofs, out of the trees, under the hedgerows. The ditches which followed the hedges along the lower roads were soon brimming with standing water, while in the fields the stone dikes and penfolds began to rise again from the snow, like the superstructure of some salvaged ship from an ocean of still whiteness.

But the lines of stone ran deep into the snow again not far up the fellside and Carpenter saw that the mountain streams, though swollen, had not yet become the hectic brown torrents of the full thaw. It would depend on the night. The spirits of the high hills were still capable of throwing a savage frost over the landscape and binding everything in its unrelenting grip for a few more days. Or even weeks.

But Carpenter prepared his gear all the same. The rope. The rubber groundsheet. The ice-axe. The short-handled spade. Everything necessary for survival.

The phone rang that night. It was Wednesday again, Mary's regular night. He had rung her back after Wilkinson's departure but got no reply. Nor the next night, and he had resolved furiously that he would not try again.

Now he seized the phone quickly from its rest.

'Mary,' he said.

'No, Mr Carpenter,' said a man's voice apologetically. 'This is Sergeant Wilkinson.'

'I'm sorry. What can I do for you?'

His voice sounded perfectly normal as far as he himself could judge. But insanely he felt tempted to press the mouthpiece to his chest so that his racing heart-beat could be heard along the line.

'If you're expecting a call, I could ring back later,' offered Wilkinson.

'No, that's all right.'

'Well, I'm sorry to trouble you, Mr Carpenter, but a thought occurred to me after I left you the other day.'

'Yes.' His tongue felt dry, a foul obstruction to his breathing.

'It's my wife really.' The man's mad, thought Carpenter. 'She's secretary of the local W.I. And when I mentioned you being a writer and that, she wondered if you would be willing to give a talk at one of their meetings. If you were going to be in the district for a little while longer, that is.'

Carpenter held his hand over the mouthpiece while he let out a long sigh that was almost a sob.

'That's very flattering,' he said. 'But I think I may be going back to London quite soon.'

'Oh. She'll be very disappointed,' said Wilkinson, adding as though it were a powerful extra argument, 'she's read some of your books.'

'Well, I'm sorry,' began Carpenter, but there was an interruption at the other end. It sounded like a radio crackling in the background and Wilkinson excused himself abruptly. He was gone a couple of minutes and Carpenter was on the point of hanging up when the sergeant's voice resumed.

'Sorry about that, sir. Another youngster's got himself into trouble and they're calling out the Mountain Rescue. Twice in a week! I'll have to take a look at things. Perhaps I could ring you in the morning to see if we can't sort something out. Goodbye now.'

He rang off before Carpenter could reinforce his refusal. Carpenter stared down at the silent phone for a few moments, wondering if Mary would ring now. Finally he shook his head and went about his business. It did not matter if she rang or not. It did not matter if he never saw her again. There was still work to be done.

It took him a long time to go to sleep that night. He lay awake listening to the steady drip of water from the roof and the perceptibly growing spate of the beck which ran down the ghyll beyond the cottage. The thaw was continuing.

It was still half dark when he set out the following morning. He would have started off even earlier but it was foolish to risk a broken ankle a quarter mile from home just for the sake of an extra half hour.

He walked steadily, following the line of the ghyll, not stopping till the misty sun had cleared the fells to the east and his cottage was the merest blob of grey paint in a Romantic landscape. Here, resting on a flat rock above the leaping, wrestling torrent of the swollen beck, he was surprised to discover how tired he was. It was a long time since he had done any steep walking.

Not since the twenty-sixth of December to be precise.

This was the way they had come. With the kind of contrived irony the subconscious mind loves, he was sitting on the very same rock they had all rested on that day. He had not been lying to Wilkinson when he described his relationship with the two of them as being based on a parity of affection. Though he had slept with Mary two or three times during some of Jack's long absences, he felt it no more of a disloyalty than the occasions when after a drinking session he ended up sharing a whore (sometimes professional, sometimes amateur) with Jack. There had been no sense of incongruity in having them to stay for Christmas and the holiday had seemed to pass very well. Mary had done the cooking and they had wined and dined in grand style. And on Boxing Day as they laboured up the fellside on the stiff walk which Carpenter insisted was a necessary counter to their celebratory excesses, they seemed joined together in a bond of friendship which Mary's adultery only made the stronger.

By early afternoon they had had enough and he left them exhausted to eat roast goose sandwiches washed down with whisky, while he vaingloriously climbed the remaining two hundred feet to add a stone to the cairn on the summit.

It had taken him longer than he anticipated and as he descended the afternoon light was fading fast, helped on its way by the dark grey clouds of a lowering sky. He began to hurry, glad of the help of the home-made alpenstock he always carried on the fells, much to his friends' amusement.

They were not at the place he had left them. For a moment he thought they must have started the descent without him. Then he saw them far over to the right, dangerously near the edge of one of the deep clefts which radiated from beneath the crest of the mountain as though in a distant age of giants an attempt had been made to split it open with huge wedges.

They were close together; embracing, he thought with a pang of jealousy which surprised him. But their movements were too violent for a mere embrace. They were struggling.

He ran towards them, calling. For a moment they paused.

'Tom !' screamed Mary. 'Help me !'

Her cry was desperate and it was cut short by Jack's fingers at her throat. He had the look of a man beyond all rational control. His eyes were dilated hugely and his face was stretched taut and bloodless, except where Mary's fingernails had drawn livid lines down his cheeks. She seemed to have lost all strength now and without thinking Carpenter raised his alpenstock and thrust at Jack with all his might. The steel ferrule caught him high on the temple, opening up a three inch gash. Releasing his wife, he turned to face Carpenter and seized the shaft of the alpenstock. His mouth worked as though he were trying to say something. Then with a sudden convulsive gesture, he wrenched the implement from Carpenter's unresisting hands, staggered back with the impetus of his own success, and, as though by a trick with a cine camera, he was gone.

'Oh Christ!' said Carpenter.

'He was trying to push me over,' sobbed Mary. 'He knew about us. He was trying to kill me.'

Jack's body lay about forty feet down, wedged deep between two jagged rocks. In his hand he still clutched the alpenstock. To scramble down within ten feet of him was relatively easy; to get further without a rope, impossible.

But from this range the ruin of his head was clear enough for no closer diagnosis to be needed.

In any case, there was no time. Mary was in a state of near collapse and the last remnants of light were being squeezed out between the grey skies and the grey rock.

Even with Carpenter's local knowledge, to be caught on the fellside in darkness could be fatal, especially with the kind of weather he felt in the air. Taking Mary by the arm, he set off down.

At first she was a burden, sobbing and protesting, but something of his urgency finally communicated itself to her and by the time the first snowflakes began to fall, they were following the line of the ghyll which ran down past the cottage. Even then it was a close call, and they were both exhausted and sodden by the time they staggered together through the black oak door.

Why he had not rung the police straightaway, he could not now precisely remember. It was all so far away, like an intimation of pre-existence. Mary had pleaded, begged, wept, collapsed, recovered, and finally, most devastatingly, submitted. He had replaced the phone and left it till morning. With the weather as it was, there was nothing to be done that night anyway, he told himself.

Even then he had a sense of glacier-like inevitability. He could find no voice to protest when Mary came to him in the night nor to argue when in the snow-light of morning she outlined her plan.

Jack had tried to kill her, she told him calmly. She felt no regrets at what had happened. Nor should Carpenter. But the police might not fully understand if they found the body with its head split open, and an easily identifiable weapon in its hands. It could mean a lot of trouble for Carpenter.

Her plan was gruesomely simple. They would recover the body together and bury it. A shallow grave somewhere remote and inaccessible, well strewn with rocks, should remain undiscovered forever. She would then return to London and establish Jack's presence there, not difficult as he had been writing a couple of business letters to be sent off on his return, and it would be fairly easy to give their circle of acquaintances the impression that Jack was around. Carpenter himself could claim to have heard from him if necessary. After a couple of weeks, she would announce they had split up and Jack had walked out on her. And as he was a man of such irregular working habits, it might take months till his disappearance caused concern.

'It's impossible!' Carpenter had told her.

'Why?' she demanded. Carpenter looked at her. She lay naked beside him in bed. Her eyes were frightened. She looked defenceless, vulnerable, her red hair spread over the pillow like a sunburst. So instead of saying it was impossible because he could not bring himself to do it, he pointed out of the window.

'The snow. We couldn't possibly get back up there in these conditions.'

She lay in thought for a moment.

'That's all right,' she had said finally. 'No one else will be able to either. If necessary I'll go back to London alone. You can stay up here and wait for the thaw. It will work very nicely.'

She ended on a triumphant note and produced such rational counters to his practical objections that in the end he was reduced to a silence which she clearly took for agreement.

Carpenter blamed himself. He had somehow let himself be cast in an unsuitable role in an absurd plot. He in no way loved Mary enough to kill for her, and he loved Jack far too much willingly to have caused him harm. Yet he realised as the weeks slipped by and the thaw never came that to the potential audience of newspaper readers, jurors, friends even, he must inevitably appear as the homicidally jealous lover in a hackneyed triangle drama. Gradually a kind of moral catalepsy set in so that he was able to contemplate his situation with a mere numb bewilderment and behave with apparent normality in an existence which had the kind of strange otherness that snow gives to the natural world.

Now the snow was going, though it had by no means all gone. He was climbing steadily up a long ridge whose sloping sides were crossed by a series of sharp undulations. The sun had not yet been able to touch the bottoms of these hollows and the snow still lay there in long thin streaks, like ribs running out from the ridge's spine.

Something caught Carpenter's eyes in one of these depressions and when he turned aside to examine it, he found himself looking at the slight, pathetic skeleton of a small animal, almost certainly a lamb. How or why its mother should have strayed so high to give birth was beyond reasoning. But its misfortune must have been a welcome relief to other ravening animals. The bones had been picked clean.

The scavengers would go no higher, Carpenter assured himself. Their natural tendency must be to make for the lower ground in such weather. The very cold itself would act as both deterrent and preservative. But for a moment he felt within a breath of turning round and going back down the mountain to whatever might ultimately await him there. But the moment passed. With a savage thrust of his foot he scattered the small skeleton down the hillside and pressed on up the ridge at a fast pace, not pausing for another hour till he found himself approaching the spot at which he had left the Yateses on Boxing Day.

Here he slowed down, finally coming to a halt at the flat boulder on which they had sat and eaten their lunch. Something gleamed among the rocks. It was a small whisky bottle, stripped of its label by the retreating snow. Absurdly Carpenter felt guilty at the thought that this was their litter, left three months earlier.

But even such feelings were mere procrastination. He turned towards the cleft in the rocky slope which lay about thirty yards to his left. Slowly he began to walk forward. It was as if he had stepped into a new dimension. Rocks, sky, wind; the sliding stones underfoot, the cold air on his face; sounds, sights, smells; all combined in a new inimical way, opening his mind wide and telling him that what lay over the edge of that stony cleft was going to rise up to meet him and cling to him for ever. There was no way of burying it here on the mountain, not really burying it. He would take it with him always as he played out his allotted role. Mary's lover. Mary's husband perhaps. Why not ? In fact, what else could happen? They were bound together now.

He came to a halt.

Here they had been struggling. Here he had stood, thrusting with his alpenstock, held lance-like.

And here Jack had stepped backwards.

He looked down.

Nothing.

Black rock, grey boulders. Snow in the crevices still. But apart from that, nothing.

He walked up and down the edge, convinced he had merely mistaken the spot. But after a few minutes he returned. There was no doubt. This was where it had happened. Right here.

Unless it had all happened only in his mind. Unless this strange frozen state he had entered during the past few weeks was merely a type of insanity producing an illusion of guilt more terrible than guilt itself.

The new dimension was still here. Sky was pressing hard down on him, trying to force him over the edge into the cleft.

Carefully he squatted down on his heels and, rocking gently to and fro, tried to work things out. It was important to do so. He knew that without doing this, there was no way for him to leave the mountainside. No way except one.

'Poor bastard,' said the doctor looking down at the body. It was the only epitaph which had been uttered so far. The climbers of the Mountain Rescue team had borne their burdened stretcher down the fellside in the exhausted, despairing silence which always accompanies the returning dead. The men waiting by the ambulance needed only a distant sighing of the party to know that there would be no breakneck drive along the valley roads to the hospital.

Now the husk of the man lay on a marble slab, his eyes still open as though trying desperately to glimpse some possible answer to an insoluble question.

With a shake of his head, the doctor began his examination.

Sergeant Wilkinson shivered as he stood in the cold living room of Carpenter's cottage. The fire had not been lit that day and the chilling damp of the outside air had quickly established itself here.

The sergeant was a big man but he moved lightly round the room, as though unwilling to disturb that silence that can fall on a house as palpably as dust. There was little sense of purpose in his movements He lifted an ornament from the mantelshelf, opened a door of the ancient dresser which filled most of one wall, riffled through some papers which lay on the bureau.

'What are you doing?' said a voice behind him.

He turned. Standing in the door was a tall red-haired woman.

He glanced non-committally at the stripes on his tunic sleeve.

'Sergeant Wilkinson,' he said. 'May I ask who you are, please ?'

'I'm Mary Yates,' said the woman. 'I'm a friend of Mr Carpenter's. Where is he?'

'Why do you want to see him, Mrs Yates?'

'Why ... I'm a friend. I just happen to be in the neighbourhood, so I thought ... Nothing's happened, has it?'

'Did Mr Carpenter know you were coming, Mrs Yates ?'

'No. I did try to ring a couple of times earlier in the day, but there was no reply. What's going on?'

'Please sit down, Mrs Yates,' said Wilkinson gently. He waited till the woman had seated herself by the cold fire.

'Mr Carpenter went out on the fells today,' he continued. 'Not a wise thing to do by yourself at this time of year.'

'Has something happened?' demanded the woman, her voice strained.

'Have you any idea what might have made him do this?' asked Wilkinson, ignoring her.

'No. Why should I? He likes walking, that's why he has a cottage up here.'

'Yes. You all went walking together at Christmas, didn't you? You and your husband and Mr Carpenter, I mean.'

There was a long silence.

'How do you know that?' she asked finally.

'How? It's no secret, is it, Mrs Yates? Didn't you tell my colleagues that when they were questioning you about your husband's disappearance?'

'Yes. Probably. It's of no consequence though I find it odd that you ... Sergeant, tell me, has Mr Carpenter had an accident?'

She sounded very urgent, but Wilkinson was slow to respond all the same.

'Accident?' he repeated. 'When you bring a body down off the fells, that's the thing most people assume. Accident. I suppose that's what you could call it.'

'Oh Jesus. Is he badly hurt?' she demanded.

'Hurt? I said "a body", Mrs Yates. I'm sorry.'

She bent forward so that her long red hair screened her face.

'Where did you find him?' she asked almost inaudibly.

'I don't know. I expect the rescue team will have the spot pin-pointed. Are you all right?'

'I'll be fine. It's just the shock.'

'Of course,' said Wilkinson sympathetically. 'And the strain of not knowing.'

'Not knowing what?' she asked warily.

'Not knowing if Mr Carpenter managed to bury your husband or not.'

She let out a long sigh, but said nothing. She opened her handbag and took out a packet of cigarettes.

'Well, you know now,' said Wilkinson. 'Is there anything you'd like to say? I must warn you that anything you do say ...'

'Spare me the tele-cop bit,' she said, lighting a cigarette and standing up. 'I don't know what this is all about. Are you trying to say that something's happened to my husband as well? Just forget the circumlocutions and tell me what's on your mind.'

'All right,' said Wilkinson. 'A working theory would be that you and Mr Carpenter were lovers and decided to get Mr Yates out of the way. So you push him over a cliff at Christmas.'

'Absurd,' she retorted quickly. 'Firstly my husband returned to London with me after the Christmas holidays. There must be ways of checking this. He wrote letters, made phone calls, that sort of thing. So if he did come back to see Tom and something happened, it's nothing to do with me. And secondly, Tom and I are not lovers.'

'Difficult to prove.' suggested Wilkinson.

'I suppose so, but there's circumstantial evidence. I'm in love with somebody else, that's true, and I have been for almost a year now. We intend getting married eventually. So Tom would hardly have joined me in a plot to get rid of Jack, would he?' she concluded triumphantly.

'Right,' said Wilkinson. 'If there *were* such a man.'

The woman thought a second, then scribbled a name and address on a page torn from her diary.

'There is,' she said. 'You can check with him, I don't mind.'

'Most co-operative,' said Wilkinson approvingly. 'So if Carpenter did harm your husband, it had nothing at all to do with you .'

'Nothing,' she said firmly. 'Absolutely nothing.'

'And the converse would be true,' pursued Wilkinson. 'I mean, if something did happen at Christmas, then Carpenter would have had no motive to be involved?'

'A pointless question,' she said. 'May I go now, please?'

'Why, yes,' said Wilkinson glancing at the door, 'I think we're all ready now.'

She turned and jerked convulsively as though she had walked into an invisible electrified barrier.

In the door, dark-suited, holding a large suitcase in his hand, was Carpenter.

'All packed then?' asked Wilkinson cheerfully. 'Good. Then there's nothing to keep us.'

'You told me he was dead,' whispered the woman.

'Never in this world!' denied the sergeant. 'I said they brought a body down off the fells. They did. But it was your husband's, Mrs Yates. The Mountain Rescue were looking for someone quite different when they found him, but they brought him back all the same. Mr Carpenter must have just missed them. It was a bit of a shock for him, I dare say, finding the cupboard bare. But fortunately he managed to work it out.'

'It doesn't make any difference,' she answered, staring fixedly at Carpenter. 'It's nothing to do with me.'

'That's not for me to decide,' said Wilkinson. 'But I think you'll need a better story, Mrs Yates. You see, the body was very well preserved. Refrigerated, you might say. And the doctor found some very interesting marks on Mr Yates's face. But more interesting still were the stomach contents. Roast goose sandwiches, he reckoned. Very Christmasy. And most interesting of all, there was evidence that he had recently imbibed a large quantity of sleeping pills, probably dissolved in some form of alcohol. A dangerous combination for a man on a mountain walk. Did you think it best to get him a bit groggy before you pushed him over? It makes it that much easier for a woman, I imagine.'

His voice was gentle, sympathetic even. The woman did not answer and Carpenter took up the thread of speech.

'But it didn't work fast enough, Mary,' he said equally gently. 'You knew I would be back soon, so you had to go ahead. And Jack was still awake enough to make a fight of it. God! No wonder you didn't want it reported as an accident! A simple broken neck might have been accepted without much fuss, but you couldn't risk the kind of post mortem they would probably give when they saw the evidence of a fight. And you said it was to protect me!'

Mary turned to Wilkinson.

'Let's go,' she said.

As they moved past Carpenter, she paused.

'You and Jack were two of a kind,' she said scornfully. 'I could have divorced him and cited you as co-respondent!'

'Why didn't you just divorce him?' murmured Wilkinson hopefully. 'Insurance?'

She ignored him.

'Just remember, Tom. He was alive when you came back. I didn't have to push him over after all, did I?'

'No. I won't forget. But I can live with it,' said Carpenter. 'I can live with it now.'

But she was gone through the door and she didn't hear. Wilkinson went after her, in close formation, like an equerry dancing attendance on a queen.

Carpenter looked round the living room. He *had* got it nice, there was no doubt about it. But he doubted if he would be back. What lay ahead was not pleasant; statements, questions, the courts; and Mary's story might still drag him down. But it could be no worse than the three snow-filled months he had just endured.

On the front step, after he had locked the big black door, he looked up at the darkening sky and listened attentively. It was good. The thaw continued. The valley was full of the sound of rushing waters.

PETER LEWIS

Peter Lewis is Emeritus Reader in English Studies at Durham University, where he has taught courses on crime fiction at BA and MA levels. In addition to a number of scholarly books on radio drama and eighteenth-century literature, he has written biographical/critical studies of John le Carré and Eric Ambler. The first won an Edgar Allan Poe Award for non-fiction in the USA, while the second was shortlisted for two American literary prizes. A member of the CWA, he has also published crime stories in various anthologies. With Margaret Lewis, he runs Flambard Press, which includes crime fiction on its list.

Peter Lewis

COUNTRY PURSUITS

A s with most things, Giles could never make up his mind about blood sports. He was pulled in opposite directions, had a foot in both camps. It all depended. There were times when the townee in him, the city boy, felt intense repugnance about killing for pleasure. Reading about the armies of French and Italian shooters who indiscriminately massacred migrating birds in their thousands to prove their machismo and for the sheer fun of it - the *fun!* - made him want to line the bastards up and then mow them down with automatic fire.

Morally, he acknowledged, this was absurdly inconsistent, but it would serve them right, the froggy, woppy gun-brigade, for blasting birds from the North, many from England indeed, out of the sky. In a sixth-form debate at school, his friend Lucas, who always liked to wind everyone up by saying the unsayable, had produced a quote from a leading postmodernist philosopher with an unpronounceable name - even worse than saying *Kierkegaard* the Danish way with glottal stops: 'If human history teaches us anything, it's that there's nothing wrong in killing people - as long as you kill the right people. The only moral problem is choosing the right people.' If those gun-crazy latins didn't qualify, who did?

Such murderous fantasies with xenophobic overtones were uncharacteristic of Giles and short-lived, but they did occur from time to time. The idea of redneck American hunters heading off to the wilds with their heavily armed sons, not long out of diapers and barely able to tie their shoe laces or buckle their belts, to bang away at anything and everything that moved, game wardens included, also made him reach for his imaginary assault rifle.

But even as he adopted the moral high ground, Giles admitted to himself that he was standing on quicksand. Why should he get stirred up over American neanderthals reverting to prehistory when animals in their millions were killed every year to feed English townees, who didn't like to think too much about battery hens, intensive farming and slaughterhouses - or abattoirs as they squeamishly preferred to call them. This was human necessity, of course, not sport, but then deer shooters argued that they were engaged on necessary culls and fox hunters on necessary pest control. Was sport, perhaps, the wrong word for what they did? Could the problem be linguistic?

In the sixth-form of his Newcastle school, fox hunting had become a fashionable issue because of parliamentary moves to ban it. The city boy in Giles understood why something as alien to the majority of his fellow-students as fox hunting seemed indefensible. Grown adults in funny outfits who should know better rollicking around the countryside on horseback with a pack of dogs to the sound of horns solely to pursue and try to kill an attractive animal which children's television had converted into a cuddly toy. Who could possibly defend that?

Well, perverse Lucas for one, the professional *enfant terrible* and *bête noire* of the upper sixth, whose determination to be different made him both stimulating and infuriating. In a discussion group at school, he came up with Ibsen's 'The minority is always right' to establish that fox hunting was a bloody good thing - and the bloodier the better. Kill the vermin. Tear and rip them to shreds. Gouge their entrails out. Hack off their tails - or whatever the horrible bushy things were called. Pull the heads off any cubs lying around with your bare hands. The Gospel according to Lucas stated that humans were by far the most predatory, destructive and death-dealing animals evolution has yet thrown up, so why pretend otherwise. Lucas was delighted that his provocative rhetoric had some of the girls in tears and others screaming for him to shut up, which only made him worse. When the teacher intervened, Lucas complained to the School Principal that this was a serious violation of his freedom of speech and of his God-given right of reply as an Englishman. Threatening to go to the European Court of Human Rights if necessary, he demanded an apology, in exchange for which he offered to be less sanguinary in future.

Even Giles berated his friend for going way over the top. Lucas, he knew, would have argued the opposite case with equal vehemence had the class approved of fox hunting. It was typical of Lucas that when they were studying *Othello*, he insisted that the title had to be a brilliant Shakespearean deception since it was obvious that Iago, the largest part and by far the cleverest character, was the hero, not the Moor of Venice whose social skills didn't go much beyond strangling his wife Desdemona. A born performer and show-off, Lucas wanted to be an actor or a barrister and whichever he chose - if there was any difference - he was going to be a great success.

While Lucas was every bit the teenage urban sophisticate, busily cultivating the *de rigeur* ironic poses of a fashionable postmodern life style, Giles was a country lad as well as a city boy. Like his father, his mother was an academic, but she came from old Durham farming stock and her brother Bob still ran the large family farm near Sedgefield in the south of the county.

During much of his childhood Giles regularly visited the farm, sometimes spending weeks at a time there so that it became a second home to him. According to Giles's father, Uncle Bob and Aunt Rose were unreconstructed country folk, and unreconstructable, too, because they rode with the local hunts as well as some in North Yorkshire. 'They'd chase a piece of string over half of England if it moved fast enough,' his father said.

Yet it suited both Giles's very ambitious parents to deposit him, their only child, at the farm so that they could, according to Uncle Bob, 'gad around the globe having holiday after holiday at the taxpayers' expense at all these international university conferences they go to, talking shop to their cronies and pretending to do important research.' Uncle Bob would say to Giles, 'You'll learn about real life with us,' implying death as well. Wandering around the countryside, Giles didn't like finding dead animals and birds, and occasionally buried them in a dignified ceremony of his own devising, but he became familiar with death at an early age, and took it for granted that farmers shot carrion and hunted foxes.

That's the way it had always been, explained Uncle Bob, so why question it. Live and let live, that was his philosophy, but oh no, that wouldn't do for the namby-pamby lily-livered self-righteous middle-class ghouls with water instead of blood in their veins who read *The Guardian* or *The Independent* or even both. They hated country pursuits and were determined to put an end to them. These people, he told Giles, knew nothing at all about rural life and the traditions of the countryside, and cared less. As far as Uncle Bob was concerned, anyone from south of the Humber was suspect, and anyone from south of Watford had to be shunned for fear of lethal contamination: 'If you get too near them, you'll catch BSE, and I don't mean New Variant CJD, I mean BSE itself.'

Whenever Giles visited the farm, he enjoyed listening to Uncle Bob's homespun rantings while taking them with a dollop of salt. It made a refreshing change from the liberal pieties of school and home and the holier-than-thou dogmas of the leftish broadsheets his parents favoured. It only took a few days there for Giles to feel a country boy again, even absorbing some of Bob's perspective since he was aware that his uncle's flamboyant outspokenness was a form of defence against increasingly hostile attitudes towards his way of life. At one time Uncle Bob called his enemies 'trendy liberals'. Now they were 'New Labourites', even dirtier words in his vocabulary. The fact that the Prime Minister was the local MP made it even worse.

As both city boy and country boy, Giles had grown up knowing at first-hand that there were at least two ways of looking at Uncle Bob's country pursuits, including hunting. By the time he reached the upper sixth, Giles realised that the ideological programme behind his impeccably liberal schooling in an environment devoted to pluralism and multiculturalism was to instil the belief that there was never one and only one way of looking at events or interpreting experience. That was the way of narrow-minded bigots whose blinkers made them blind to reality. Some of the current-affairs classes at school about the political problems facing countries like Northern Ireland, Israel and South Africa made all this abundantly clear.

No, there were always different angles on things. Indeed, so many, at times, that you couldn't talk about two sides to every question. There were far more than that. On the one hand... But on the other... And then there's another... And another... And another... There were hands everywhere, as on those carvings of Hindu goddesses or temple dancing girls or whatever they were. Duty-bound to see other points of view meant that coming to a conclusion or making a decision about anything was virtually out of the question. Could any opinion be more than a personal whim? Was objective truth a dangerous illusion - an impossible straw clutched at by people who still naively yearned for certainties that didn't exist?

And yet, on the other hand... At school they did discuss issues on which there was total unanimity. About nuclear weapons and anti-personnel landmines, there was only one hand, especially after Princess Diana's death. The Holocaust, too, seemed to produce no other hands, until Lucas, always out to shock delicate sixth-form sensibilities, especially the girls', caused a furore by raising the possibility of viewing it from a Nazi perspective: 'Not only was it an extraordinarily bold imaginative project that would have seemed mission impossible to most people, it was amazingly successful considering the short time they had to implement it.' Even Lucas felt he had gone a bit far this time, especially with a couple of Jews in the class. Compared with genocide, weapons of mass destruction, and world-wide environmental destruction, fox hunting seemed almost trivial, and although virtually all the sixth formers were opposed to it, some were willing to concede that there was - but only just - another hand and weren't sure that their disapproval warranted a total ban. With opinion polls indicating that on the whole the population favoured the restoration of capital punishment, which they, *pace* Lucas, regarded as an abomination, they agreed that one had to be very wary about the dictatorship of the majority. Lucas, of course, wanted to hang, shoot, guillotine, gas, electrocute or lethally inject - and preferably all six simultaneously - anyone found guilty of anything, without the possibility of an appeal. In public and on TV.

As soon as he'd finished his A-levels, Giles went down to the farm to recover. There hadn't been time for more than fleeting visits since the previous summer. With his father looking over one shoulder, his mother over the other, and both breathing down his neck, he'd worked very hard in the upper sixth and had never felt so exhausted. He needed a break and was also glad to get away from his sixth-form girlfriend Louise for a while. She was in a state of neurotic panic about the exams, moping on about about how badly she'd done and how she wouldn't be able to go to Cambridge, when everyone knew that if she didn't receive top grades in all her subjects the examiners would need to have their own heads examined. Louise could be a pain at times.

Giles enjoyed a few days of idleness, swimming, sunbathing and sleeping, before Uncle Bob and his black-sheep son Matthew suggested a thoroughly deserved treat - a reward for his academic efforts. He hadn't been to stay on the farm for ages, they said, so he needed to be treated like the Prodigal Son. They didn't have a fatted calf handy, but they might be able to provide something more to his taste.

The next day they loaded him into their new Range Rover, going he knew not where or why, but suspecting that their mysterious destination had something to do with blood sports. Nothing as commonplace as fox hunting, either. There had been hints about the outing, but when Giles asked Uncle Bob and Matthew what they were planning, their replies were of the 'Wait and see' or 'You'll soon find out' variety accompanied by sinister laughs. 'It would spoil it for you if you knew in advance, so don't ask,' Matthew told him. 'It'll be a nice surprise. After all your swotting, you need a different course of instruction. It's high time you were blooded, so to speak.' Giles knew Matthew well enough to know that if he called something 'nice' it was probably anything but. And *blooded* sounded ominous.

According to Giles's parents, Uncle Bob should have been much firmer with Matthew during his adolescence, but whenever Giles went to stay on the farm, he thought that father and son were two of a kind. Because Matthew had been such a mischievous youth and had somehow managed to avoid expulsion from university and even obtain a degree in agriculture despite being a drunken rowdy for his entire three years there, Giles's parents often called him his Bad Cousin Matthew. But as far as Giles was concerned, Matthew was a chip off the old block. You might just as well label Bob, Bad Uncle Bob.

As a young boy, Giles didn't play very much with Matthew, who was several years older, much bigger and usually with friends his own age from the nearby village. Giles thoroughly enjoyed himself traipsing around with Uncle Bob, trying to avoid making a nuisance of himself. Aunt Rose didn't keep too close an eye on him since when she wasn't in the office looking after the business side of the farm, she was racing around the countryside, hobnobbing with the local gentry, arranging fundraising events for the local church, or, in Uncle Bob's words, 'meddling in some damn thing or another - a finger in every pie, your Aunt Rose. Typical woman.'

It was only when Matthew was in his teens that he involved Giles in the bizarre games he devised with his friends, including sadistic ones like Pirates, which involved pitched battles in the haystack followed by floggings with an improvised cat-o'-nine-tails, plank-walking on the diving board, and even a version of keel-hauling in the swimming pool.

Matthew made it clear to Giles that it was a great privilege for him to join in such *sports* - he didn't call them games - and that he'd better not say anything about them to Aunt Rose or Matthew's sisters or he'd be tossed naked into a large bed of nettles. It didn't matter about Uncle Bob. He didn't mind what they got up to as long as no one was killed or injured. Except at mealtimes, in fact, Giles didn't see all that much of the two girls, deeply involved in love affairs with their ponies. If they weren't riding they were grooming them, and Aunt Rose seemed to take them to every gymkhana under the sun - more often under the clouds in the North-East. At that age Giles had little contact with girls outside school and they didn't interest him, although Matthew showed him what he could look forward to when a little older by producing glossy magazines, stolen from the top shelf of a newsagent's shop, displaying lots of tits, bums, and open crotches.

For several years when Matthew was a student, Giles barely saw him. Matthew was either at university, doing a placement somewhere as part of his studies, or backpacking his way around the world. But now that Matthew was back, helping his father to run the farm, Giles's relationship with him was totally different from when he was a turbulent teenager. Going to the pub replaced Matthew's imaginative if sometimes brutal games as the main entertainment.

And it was in a pub with Uncle Bob and Matthew a couple of days after returning to the farm that Giles overheard his Bad Cousin whispering to another young farmer, Brian, that there was about to be another 'chase'. Or was it 'race'? Whatever it was, it was 'usual time, usual place'. Giles had no idea what was meant and didn't ask. He knew better than to pry into farmers' secrets, but thinking that it was a confidence shared only by the two young farmers, he was surprised when Uncle Bob went over to Brian as he was leaving and said, 'See you at the you know what. You'll be there, won't you?'

On the following day, with more talk of the Return of the Prodigal, both Uncle Bob and Matthew dropped a few hints about involving Giles in something special, but mum's the word as far as Aunt Rose and the girls were concerned. 'Men's stuff,' said Matthew, 'and don't give me any of your PC crap. As far as I'm concerned, there are still only two types of women: virgins and whores. You marry the first and you screw the second until their pips squeak.' Giles wasn't much more than a virgin himself, although he wouldn't have admitted it to Matthew.

Louise wasn't unwilling exactly, but neither was she enthusiastic or even co-operative, so they never managed to be in a convenient place at a convenient time. Lucas called her the kind of girl who says she's ready for sex as long as she can keep her tights and knickers on - and her legs pressed together. It was girls like her, he told Giles during one of their English A-level classes, that T.S. Eliot's Sweeney had in mind when he said, 'Any man has to, needs to, wants to Once in a lifetime, do a girl in.' Giles at moments knew the feeling. There'd been a few messy splodgings on the back seat of her mother's car, and some breezy al fresco endeavours in Jesmond Dene with Louise more concerned about grass stains on her skirt than the job in hand - in her hands, actually. When Giles was aroused, she tended to break into a fit of the giggles, so he felt like slapping her face to shut her up, or spanking her bum, or even damn well forcing the little bitch to teach her a lesson. The desire to attack her subsided quickly but was real enough while it lasted. A few times he had grabbed her hard and almost become violent, but seeing how anxious she'd looked he'd backed off and apologised.

Giles's only other experiences had been with Karen, a somewhat older medical student who'd seduced him at a party. A woman, not a girl, she certainly knew a thing or three, and didn't even bother with underwear, not at parties anyway, but she frightened as well as fascinated him. Dominant and assertive, a bit of a sexual bully, she was totally different from Louise, yet perhaps she too would have made Sweeney have to, need to, want to do her in. Her extraordinary control and self-confidence certainly made Giles want to fight back, even hurt her. Especially when it became clear that she got a particular kick from deflowering teenage boys. If there were female paedophiles, Giles thought, weird Karen was close to being one. He hoped she wasn't going to specialise in paediatrics.

Before setting off in the Range Rover, Uncle Bob told Aunt Rose that he was taking the boys out for a bar meal and a game of darts with some farmers down Sadberge way so they would be gone for a while. But it was soon obvious to Giles that they hadn't taken the right road. Perhaps they were going to pick somebody up en route, but when he asked, Matthew said, 'Who do you fancy picking up, Giles? A busty hitchhiker with her skirt up to her arse? Don't worry about it. We won't have to do any picking up today. The fruit's already picked.'

This only added to the mystery Bob and Matthew had been generating with their earlier veiled remarks about blooding and an unusual country pursuit. What could it be? Giles tried to imagine what needed to be kept so secret. Some sort of shoot? Nothing unusual about that for Uncle Bob and Matthew, unless they were after an endangered species. And how many of those were there in County Durham? In any case, father and son were surprisingly good about conservation, refraining from grubbing up hedgerows on their land for example, and there was no sign of guns in the vehicle. Badger digging? Definitely not their scene. Matthew had once given a badger digger a ferocious beating and was lucky not to be charged with GBH. Bear-baiting? Hardly. Even if they were capable of it, where would they find a bear? Dog fighting? Remotely possible, but they were very English about dogs and actively disliked the very aggressive breeds like Pit Bulls. Cock fighting? Perhaps a bit more likely, but while he could imagine them hunting big game he really couldn't see them getting a kick out of a couple of birds going at each other hammer and tongs. No, he would just have to be patient and do what they said: wait and see.

From his knowledge of the area, Giles was trying to work out where they were heading, along narrow country roads and then a long dirt track before ending up in a meadow beside a stream at the bottom of a gentle grassy slope. This was why they'd come in the four-wheel drive rather than one of the cars they usually used on good roads. He'd been wondering about the choice of vehicle. It was a remote spot almost surrounded by woods, and the nearest house was some distance away, far out of sight. Several four-wheel drives and a large car with heavily tinted glass were already parked in the field and a number of men were busy putting what looked like markers on the ground.

It was still very warm in the early evening - perfect conditions for a country pursuit, according to Matthew as they walked across to greet the others. 'You're late, Bob,' said a pink-cheeked middle-aged man with a beer belly, 'almost missed the fun. Given you up for lost. We've drawn lots already, so you'll have to wait your turn.'

'Had to settle the wife and daughters down in front of the TV before they asked any questions,' said Uncle Bob. 'Is everyone here?'

'Everyone who's coming.'

'Including the Prime Minister, I suppose,' Uncle Bob grinned.

'That'll be the day. When his wife lets him out of her sight. Would do him the world of good, though. Spending your life in 10 Downing Street and the House of Commons would damage anyone's mental health. Now who's this?' the roly-poly man asked, shaking Giles's hand. 'Your grandson?'

'Grandson, indeed!' roared Uncle Bob. 'He's Giles, my sister's boy. How old do you think I am?'

'Not too old for a chase, although I suppose you'll leave that to the young ones and just watch, you old voyeur,' came the reply, and the two farmers moved off to talk to a few others who were swigging from hip flasks. Whisky, probably, thought Giles, but it could be that tipple popular with hunters and shooters, King's Ginger Liqueur. Uncle Bob gave him a warming glass sometimes.

Turning to Matthew, Giles said, 'Now we're here, wherever it is, tell me what's going on. What kind of chase did he mean?'

'Can't you guess? Well, the meadow's a kind of racing track, only we call it the course, of course.' Matthew chuckled.

So that was it. Course. Coursing. Matthew had used the word before, but Giles hadn't registered the implication. Coursing hares. Why hadn't he thought of that possibility? Probably because he'd never heard any mention of it during his visits to the farm. Even so, if he'd been daft enough to think of bear-baiting, he should have remembered coursing. Presumably the hares had been rounded up from somewhere and were in the cages or boxes in the four-wheel drives. But where were the dogs? He couldn't see any in the meadow and Uncle Bob hadn't brought any. Perhaps he wasn't expected to if he'd only come to watch, as the man implied. Yet looking around Giles couldn't see any canine faces pressed against car widows. Were they in cages, too?

All he knew about coursing was that dogs chased hares and made short work of them if they caught them, so he asked Matthew.

'So it's hare coursing you think we're about, is it? Well there's not much to hare coursing really,' he replied. 'You release one along a run, give it a chance to get away, then let a pair of hounds after it, always a pair. If it's fast enough, it reaches a safe area on the other side and lives to run another course. If it doesn't...' He signalled having his throat cut. 'Curtains. But some do get away. Quite a few. You don't fancy it, do you, young Giles? I can tell by the look on your face. But it's much fairer than what happens to bulls in Spain, the land of pain. Once they're in the ring or the corrida, if that's what the dagos call it, there's no way out except dead. Nasty lot, down there on the Costas.' He passed Giles his hip-flask. 'Have a good swig of whatever Dad's filled it with. If it's not The Macallan it'll be Glensomethingorother.'

As he drank, Giles recalled the recent shock he'd experienced when he learned that the great Spanish poet Federico García Lorca had strongly defended bullfighting as integral to Spanish culture. There'd just been a festival at the Newcastle Playhouse to celebrate Lorca's life and work, as 1998 was the centenary of his death - his martyrdom at the hands of the fascists, rather, as a gay, a poet and a radical. So how could someone like that not only tolerate but actively support bull fights at a time when most of his fellow Republicans and left-wingers, it seemed, were intent on abolishing it as a barbaric relic from a reactionary past with no place in the new Spain they were going to create?

Yet - and there was always a *yet* - using the one-hand-other-hand principle there was probably a case of sorts to be made for bullfighting. He imagined Lucas waxing lyrical about the guts of disembowelled horses spilling onto the sand, matadors gored in unmentionable places, and rivers of bulls' blood filling the corrida.

'We're about to begin the first course, the starter,' said Matthew. 'So let's go over to the starting line to see the starter start it off.' Giles groaned. Typical Matthew patter.

As they strolled to where a few men were standing, the car with heavily tinted glass pulled up and one of them opened a door. To Giles's amazement, out stepped a young woman. The door was quickly shut behind her but not before he glimpsed more people inside. Since this was supposed to be such a masculine affair, what on the earth was she doing here? And why didn't the others in the car come and watch, too?

Giles knew that plenty of women followed hunts, so there was no obvious reason why they shouldn't attend a coursing, as long as it wasn't a criminal offence. He thought hare coursing might be but simply didn't know. If it were illegal, this would explain all the secrecy about their expedition. He couldn't imagine Aunt Rose, who shot plenty of game birds in the season, being squeamish about killing a few hares, but she was a JP. The puzzling thing about the young woman standing beside the markers was that she didn't look remotely like the girlfriend or daughter of one of the huntin', shootin' and fishin' brotherhood. Wearing a skin-tight, flimsy top, a short frilly skirt and high-heeled shoes, she might have been on her way to a Newcastle club on a Friday night. The last thing she was dressed for was an occasion like this, and close-to Giles saw that despite her flashy make-up she couldn't have been older than Louise. She might still be at school.

'You look as though you've never seen a girl before,' said Matthew. 'You're not seeing things. You haven't had that much Malt. She is real.'

The man Matthew called the starter was speaking to the girl. 'You've done this before, so you know what to do.' She nodded, unsmiling and looking ill-at-ease. 'OK? We're ready and set,' he added. 'Now go!'

And she went, running awkwardly over the grass until she slowed down to kick her shoes into the air one by one before catching them, then continued running in her stockinged feet towards the sanctuary markers, quite nimbly in the circumstances. Turning to two rather paunchy men in their thirties, the starter called out, 'One, two, three, go,' and off they too went, in pursuit of the girl. To shouts of encouragement from the bystanders, they made up ground but not enough to catch her in time. Puffing and panting, they returned to the starter, complaining that he had given the prey, as they called her, too much of a lead, but he replied, 'Less beer, more speed. Don't blame me.'

Giles could hardly believe what he'd seen. Nothing had prepared him for this. Was it some kind of ritual that preceded the coursing proper? He didn't think so. It was insane, like something out of a surrealist film by Buñuel. The men had looked ludicrous, but the girl... There was something exciting about her. Fleeing the men, her skirt bouncing around her thighs, she appeared to be a figure from an erotic fantasy, vulnerable yet provocative. He tried to imagine himself chasing Louise, catching her, pulling her to the ground. Some hope. If he proposed anything like that, she'd only giggle. Or fuss about getting grass stains on her clothes.

'I thought you said this was going to be hare coursing,' Giles said to Matthew. 'Why didn't you warn me?'

'I didn't want you to get too excited in advance. Anyway I didn't mention hares. You were the one who asked about hares. This is her-coursing, Giles. Coursing hers. Haven't you caught on yet? You with all the brains.'

'You might have told me. I'd no idea anything like this went on. What would have happened if they'd caught her?'

'Not much chance of that with those fat oafs, was there? But next time she goes, she won't get such a start and somebody'll catch her. You, maybe. But if beginner's luck has anything to do with it, you'll strike lucky and have Jezebel. Let's go over to the other side for the next course and watch them coming towards us. It's better.'

Giles wasn't sure what to do. To extricate himself from the coursing now would be difficult, and he wasn't sure that he wanted to. There was a fascination in what was going to happen next. It was like watching the porn videos Lucas obtained from somewhere or the hard stuff on the Internet he also had a talent for locating. Some of the things the participants did to one another were disgusting, and the action was predictable and monotonous, but Giles couldn't take his eyes off the screen even though he knew it was way beyond the PC pale. A crime against women, according to the sixth-form feminists.

By the time they had crossed the meadow, another girl had emerged from the car, in torn jeans, a minuscule halter top and open sandals, again with high heels. She didn't look any older than the first one, and Giles found it difficult to believe that girls his own age were involved in something like this. The process of her-coursing was repeated with the same result, although it was much closer this time since the two pursuers were a bit younger and fitter. Consequently the chase was more dramatic, especially from the position Giles and Matthew were in. Matthew was right about watching the three figures running straight towards you, seeing the expressions on their faces. This time Giles was half-hoping that the girl would be caught. He wanted to see what happened next.

'Third time lucky - or unlucky - depending on your point of view,' said Matthew, as a little later another woman climbed out of the car, wearing a see-through blouse and a skirt that seemed too tight for running.

Giles asked, 'Where are they from, these…?'

'Young ladies, do you mean? Teesside's full of tarts, especially Middlesbrough. Apart from drinking, there's not much else to do in the towns around here, Darlington, Stockton, Billingham. The queues outside the massage parlours in Middlesbrough are longer than those for the Tower of London in August. You can hardly walk along the pavements for the queues. Believe me. Easy money for the ladies, and they'll do anything for sixty quid, and less if you settle for something less than anything. They earn a bit extra for coursing, that's why they enjoy it so much. Almost as much as we do. And after all the smoke and smells of Middlesbrough they really appreciate clean, fresh air. Keeps them healthy, that, and the running.'

From a distance, the way the third woman moved and stood suggested she was a bit older than the others, less gauche and awkward, more sure of herself. As soon as the course began, she pulled the skirt up high to free her legs and sprinted away. She was nearly across the field when she tripped, nearly fell but managed to regain her balance. The loss of momentum, however, allowed her two pursuers to tackle her to the ground just short of the sanctuary markers. What followed was a violent struggle with the woman shouting and twisting and turning and kicking and punching as first her blouse was torn off and then her skirt. She put up such resistance that she even succeeded in breaking free, but not for long.

Noticing that Giles was looking bothered while gazing intently, Matthew said, 'Don't worry, Giles boy, she's not a damsel in distress hoping for a knight in armour to rescue her. It isn't real, it's all part of the show. And she's brilliant, this one. Knows how to get the blood pounding. The thrill of the chase.'

Where she had finally collapsed across the field, the woman was no longer putting up a fight and the three bodies became entwined in ways Giles had seen on Lucas's videos. Only these weren't sanitised images on a screen. This was no-holds-barred rutting in 3D not intended for watching.

Matthew said, 'Leave them to it. Out of sight, out of mind. Have another tot of Glenallan or Macfiddich or whatever.' He handed Giles the flask. 'The buzz must be reaching you by now.'

Giles didn't reply, but it was. He was beginning to experience a release from all restraint, all inhibition. He thought of Louise. What an uptight prig she could be. Why couldn't she let go even once in a while? And Karen. There was something calculated about her sensuality, her seductiveness. It was contrived, put on. What was happening here was crude and primitive but also liberating and elemental. Atavistic would have been Lucas's word. It was like those comic strips about wild, bearded cavemen with large clubs in their hands chasing naked women. 'Any man has to, needs to, wants to Once in a lifetime, do a girl in.'

Giles saw Uncle Bob waving to them and then Matthew was marching him across the meadow to the starter, who was agreeing to Uncle Bob's request to give the young lad a turn before he exploded.

'You're next, Giles,' said Matthew. 'Well we are, but I'll leave it to you. It can be your baptism and first communion all in one.'

'I can't. It's out of the question. Not in front of these people.'

'But you could if no one was watching, is that it? Course you can do it, course you can run a course. And you don't have to catch her, if you're not up to it. If you're not man enough, you can let her escape. Have another tot and you'll be ready for anything.'

'I don't fancy any of them, I just don't.' Giles turned and noticed another girl sliding out of the car, wearing a low-cut sleeveless white mini-dress. For a moment he thought that she was the black supermodel who was always on TV. But no, of course she wasn't. She wasn't that pretty or that tall, but there was a resemblance. He just stood gazing at her as though hypnotised. He knew a number of girls of Asian origin in Newcastle, but none from the Caribbean. The Windrush generation hadn't migrated as far north as Tyneside. This girl beside him, reaching out to touch his arm, represented a new experience.

'This is Jezebel,' said Matthew. 'Or Jez, or Jaz, or Jade. You change your name as often as your kit, don't you Jez? What little there is of it.'

She smiled at Giles, her eyes fixed on his, and began to chat. The three previous 'hers' had looked aloof rather than friendly, but Jez seemed relaxed, almost as though this trip to the country might be her idea of fun rather than business.

'I'm glad it's you two,' she said, 'not a couple of droopers with bulging beer bellies. And if you do catch me, don't worry, you won't catch anything from me. Clean as a whistle, that's Jez.'

The starter went through his routine and she was away followed after a few seconds by Matthew who was pulling Giles by the arm. 'Now run,' shouted Matthew, 'you mustn't miss this opportunity.' And Giles, the whisky going to his head, found himself beside Matthew until his cousin took what looked like a deliberate tumble before urging him on, 'It's up to you now, Giles. Go. Chase. Pursue.'

Jez had been offered to him as his prey and he was tracking her closely, gaining ground without making a determined effort to close the gap before she reached sanctuary, as he knew he could if he tried. He was going to nearly catch her but let her escape at the last moment. That would have to satisfy Matthew and the others, who were now cheering him on. Running, he did feel somewhat woozy after the whisky, and he could blame that for his failure. But then Jez slowed down, gave him a come-hither look over her shoulder, and waggled her index finger at him. By making it impossible for him not to catch her, she had ceased playing according to the rules, and just before the sanctuary markers she came to a complete stop. Slowing down, Giles walked towards her.

'Come on, slowcoach,' she said. 'Will this help?' She unzipped the back of her dress, and instead of crossing the line she turned left and ran down the meadow towards the stream.

At that moment Giles decided that he had been duped. He had been set up, he thought, set up by Uncle Bob, Matthew, and Jezebel, probably with the complicity of the others, to provide a display for them, to make an exhibition of himself. He was the new boy ripe for initiation, the innocent lured into a ceremony of carnality as a form of entertainment. Jez was making a fool of him, tantalising him, teasing him, toying with him. They were all having fun at his expense. Fun. He would give them fun all right. If they wanted a lively show, he would provide one. They would get more than they expected. And although slightly dizzy, he ran after her, this time with determination.

He soon drew level with her and, grabbing her round the waist, he pushed her violently to the ground so that she fell awkwardly, face down.

'Take it easy,' she said. 'There's no need to be so rough. I'm not a hare. You're not supposed to tear me to shreds. Only my dress, if you want. Go on, rip it. I don't care.'

'You don't mind grass stains, then.'

'What do you mean?' she said, rising to her knees and beginning to crawl away from him, the shoulder straps of the dress falling down her arms, but he suddenly swung her onto her back and sat on her chest, pinioning her with his knees and hands.

'Let go,' she said. 'There's no need for this. You're hurting me. Now you've caught me, I'm not going to run away. I'm yours to do what you like with.'

Giles tightened his grip. In an effort to free herself, she began to twist and turn, kicking and wriggling, but using his weight he managed to hold her down. She might have looked like a million dollars when she got out of the car, but she was a slutty whore, wasn't she, nothing more. And he moved his hands to her throat, pressing, squeezing. Her hands released, she lashed out at his face with her long nails, drawing blood from his cheeks and lips. He nearly let go of her neck to slap and punch her, but he couldn't bring himself to mark her face. Instead he tightened his grip and adjusted his position to make it more difficult for her to lacerate him. Drops of blood fell onto her face from his as she tried desperately to wrench his hands from her throat.

Behind his back, Giles could hear people running towards him. Uncle Bob was shouting, 'That's enough, Giles, stop it,' and Matthew, 'Let her go, leave go.' But Giles didn't. He squeezed even harder. She wasn't struggling as much now, her hands were losing their grip on his, and her eyes looked odd. Her gasps became no more than whispers.

Giles felt hands on both his shoulders as Uncle Bob and Matthew reached him and tried to pull him away from her. But he kept pressing, squeezing, choking. They were shouting at him, hauling him back, and Matthew put his arm round his neck to lever him off, but he still didn't let go. He kept pressing, squeezing, pressing, squeezing.

VAL McDERMID

(Photo: Jerry Bauer)

Val McDermid grew up in a Scottish mining community and then read English at Oxford. Her career as a journalist ended with a three-year stint as Northern Bureau Chief of a national Sunday tabloid. She is now a full-time writer and the author of successful series featuring respectively Lindsay Gordon and the Mancunian private eye Kate Brannigan. Her non-series novel *The Mermaids' Singing* won the CWA Macallan Gold Dagger in 1995 and has been followed by *The Wire In The Blood*.

Val McDermid

GUILT TRIP

A s neither of my parents was too bothered about religion, I managed to miss out on Catholic guilt. Then I found myself working with Shelley. A guilt trip on legs, our office manager. If she treats her two teenagers like she treats me, those kids are going to be in therapy for years. 'You play, you pay,' she said sweetly, pushing the new case file towards me for the third time.

'Just because I *play* computer games doesn't mean I'm qualified to deal with the nerds who write them,' I protested. It was only a white lie; although my business partner Bill Mortensen deals with most of the work we do involving computers, I'm not exactly illiterate. I pushed the file back towards Shelley. 'It's one for Bill.'

'Bill's too busy. You know that,' Shelley said. 'Anyway, it's not software as such. It's either piracy or industrial sabotage and that's your forte.' The file slid back to me.

'Sealsoft are Bill's clients.' Brannigan's last stand.

'All the more reason you should get to know them.'

I gave in and picked up the file. Shelley gave a tight little smile and turned back to her computer screen. One of these days I'm going to get the last word. Just wait till hell freezes over. On my way out of the door and down the stairs I browsed the file. Sealsoft was a local Manchester games software house. They'd started off back in the dawn of computer gaming in the mid-eighties, writing programmes for a whole range of hardware. Some of the machines they produced games for had never been intended as anything other than word processors, but Sealsoft had grabbed the challenge and come up with some fun stuff. The first platform game I'd ever played, on a word processor that now looked as antique as a Model T Ford, had been a Sealsoft game.

They'd never grown to rival any of the big players in the field but somehow Sealsoft had always hung in there, coming up every now and again with seemingly simple games that became classics. In the last year or two they'd managed to win the odd film tie-in licence, and their latest acquisition was the new Arnold Schwarzenegger-Bruce Willis boys 'n' toys epic. But now, two weeks before the game was launched, they had a problem. And when people have problems, Mortensen and Brannigan is where they turn if they've got sense and cash enough.

I had a ten o'clock appointment with Sealsoft's boss. Luckily I could get there on foot, since parking round by Sealsoft is a game for the terminally reckless. The company had started off on the top floor of a virtually derelict canalside warehouse that had since been gutted and turned into expansive and expensive studio flats where the marginally criminal rubbed shoulders with the marginally legitimate lads from the financial services industries. Sealsoft had moved into modern premises a couple of streets away from the canal but the towpath was still the quickest way to get from my office in Oxford Road to their concrete pillbox in Castlefield.

Fintan O'Donohoe had milk-white skin and freckles so pale it looked like he'd last seen daylight somewhere in the nineteenth century. He looked about seventeen, which was slightly worrying since I knew he'd been with the company since it started up in 1983. Add that to the red-rimmed eyes, and I felt like I'd stumbled into *Interview with the Vampire*. 'Call me Fin' he said, with no trace of any accent other than pure Mancunian as we settled in his chrome and black leather office, each of us clutching our designer combinations of mineral water, herbs and juices.

I resisted the invitation. It wasn't the hardest thing I'd done that day. 'I'm told you have a problem,' I said.

'That's not the word I'd use,' he sighed. 'A major disaster waiting to happen is what we've got. We've got a boss money-earner about to hit the streets and our whole operation's under threat.'

'From what?' I asked.

'It started about six weeks ago. There were just one or two at first, but we've had getting on for sixty in the last two days. It's a nightmare,' O'Donohoe told me earnestly, leaning forward and fiddling anxiously with a pencil.

'What exactly are we talking about here?' He might not have anything better to do than take a long tour round the houses, but I certainly did. Apart from anything else, there was a cappuccino at the Atlas café with my name on it.

'Copies of our games with the right packaging, the right manuals, the guarantee cards, everything, are being returned to us because the people who buy them are shoving the disks into their computers and finding they're completely blank. Nothing on them at all. Just bog-standard, high-density preformatted unbranded three-and-a-half-inch disks.' He threw himself back in his chair, pouting like a five-year-old.

'Sounds like pirates,' I said. 'Bunch of schneid merchants copying your packaging and stuffing any old shit in there.'

He shook his head. 'My first thought. But that's not how the pirates work. They bust your copy protection codes, make hundreds of copies of the program and stuff it inside pretty crudely copied packaging. This is the opposite of that. There's no game, but the packaging is perfect. It's ours.' He opened a drawer in his desk and pulled out a box measuring about eight inches by ten and a couple of inches deep. The cover showed an orc and a human in mortal combat outlined in embossed silver foil. O'Donohoe opened the box and tipped out a game manual, a story-book, four disks with labels reading I-4 and a guarantee card. 'Right down to the hologram seal on the guarantee, look,' he pointed out.

I leaned forward and picked up the card, turning it to check the hologram. He was right. If this was piracy, I'd never seen quality like it. And if they could produce packaging like this, I was damn sure they could have copied the game too. So why the combination of spot-on packaging and blank disks? 'Weird,' I said.

'You're not kidding.'

'Is this happening to any of your competitors?'

'Not that I've heard. And I would have heard, I think.'

Sounded as if one of Sealsoft's rivals was paying off an insider to screw O'Donohoe's operation into the deck. 'Where are the punters buying them? Market stalls?' I asked.

Head down, O'Donohoe said 'Nope.' For the first time I noted dark shadows under his eyes. 'They're mostly coming back to us via the retailers, though some are coming direct.'

'Which retailers? Independents or chains?' I was sitting forward in my seat now, intrigued. What had sounded like a boring piece of routine was getting more interesting by the minute. Call me shallow and superficial, but I like a bit of excitement in my day.

'Mostly smallish independents, but increasingly we're getting returns from the big chain stores now. We've been in touch with quite a few of the customers as well, and they're all saying that the games were shrink-wrapped when they bought them.'

I sat back, disappointed. The shrink-wrapping was a clincher. 'It's an inside job,' I said flatly. 'Industrial sabotage.'

'No way,' O'Donohue said, two pale pink spots suddenly burning on his cheekbones.

'I'm sorry. I know it's the message no employer wants to hear. But it's clearly an inside job.'

'It can't be,' he insisted bluntly. 'Look, I'm not a dummy. I've been in this game a while. I know the wrinkles. I know how piracy happens. And I guard against it. Our boxes are printed in one place, our booklets in another, our guarantee cards in a third. The disks get copied in-house on to disks that are overprinted with our logo and the name of the game, so you couldn't just slip in a few blanks like these,' he said contemptuously, throwing the disks across the desk.

'Where does it all come together?' I asked.

'We're a small company,' he answered obliquely. 'But that's not the only reason we pack by hand rather than on a production line. I know where we're vulnerable to sabotage, and I've covered the bases. The boxes are packed and sealed in shrink-wrap in a room behind the despatch room.'

'Then that's where your saboteur is.'

His lip curled. 'I don't think so. I've only got two workers in there. We've always had a policy of employing friends and family at Sealsoft. The packers are my mum and her sister, my auntie Geraldine. They'd kill anybody that was trying to sabotage this business, take my word for it. When they're not working, the door's double-locked. They wouldn't even let the parish priest in there, believe me.'

'So what exactly do you want me to do?' I asked.

'I don't want you questioning my staff,' he said irritably. 'Other than that, it's up to you. You're the detective. Find out who's putting the shaft in, then come back and tell me.'

When I left Sealsoft ten minutes later, all I had to go on was a list of customers and companies involved in returns of Sealsoft's games and details of who'd sent back what. I was still pretty sure the villain was inside the walls rather than outside, but the client wasn't letting me anywhere near his good Catholic mother and auntie Geraldine. Can't say I blamed him.

I figured there wasn't a lot of point in starting with the chain stores. Even if something hooky was going on, they were the last people I could lean on to find out. With dole queues still nudging the three-million mark, the staff there weren't going to tell me anything that might cost them their jobs. I sat in the Atlas over the coffee I'd promised myself and read through the names. At first glance, I didn't recognize any of the names of the computer suppliers. We buy all our equipment and consumables by mail order, and the only shop we've ever used in dire emergencies was the one that used to occupy the ground floor of our building before it became a supermarket.

Time for some expert help. I pulled out my mobile and rang my tame darkside hacker, Gizmo. By day he works for Telecom as a systems manager. By night, he becomes the Scarlet Pimpernel of cyberspace. Or so he tells me. 'Giz? Kate.'

'Not a secure line,' he grumbled 'you should know better.'

'Not a problem. This isn't confidential. Do you know anybody who works at any of these outlets?' I started to read out the list with Gizmo grunting negatively after each name. About halfway through the list he stopped me.

'Wait a minute. That last one, Epic PC?'

'You know someone there?'

'I don't but you do. It's wossname, the geezer that used to have that place under your office.'

'Deke? He went bust, didn't he?'

''S right. Bombed. Went into liquidation, opened up a new place in Prestwich a week later, didn't he? That's his shop. Epic PC. I remember because I thought it was such a crap name. That it?'

'That'll do nicely, Giz.' I was speaking to empty air. I like a man who doesn't waste my time. I drained my cup, walked up the steps to Deansgate station and jumped the next tram to Prestwich.

Epic PC was a small shop on the main drag through Prestwich village. I recognized the special-offer stickers. It looked like Deke Harper didn't have the kind of fresh ideas that would save Epic PC from its predecessor's fate. I pushed open the door and an electric buzzer vibrated in the stuffy air. Deke himself was seated behind a PC in the middle of a long room that was stuffed with hardware and software, fingers clattering over the keys. He'd trained himself well in the art of looking busy; he let a whole five seconds pass between the buzzer sounding and his eyes leaving the screen in front of him. When he registered who his customer was, his eyebrows climbed in his narrow face. 'Hello,' he said uncertainly, pushing his chair back and getting to his feet, 'stranger.'

'Believe me, Deke, it gets a lot stranger still,' I said drily.

'You live out this way, then?' he asked nervously, hitting a key to clear his screen as I drew level with him.

'No,' I said. Sometimes it's more fun to let them come to you.

'You were passing?'

'No.' I leaned against his desk. His eyes kept flicking between me and his uninformative screen.

'You needed something for the computer? Some disks?'

'Three in a row, Deke. You lose. My turn now. I'm here about these moody computer games you've been selling. Where are they coming from?'

A thin blue vein in his temple seemed to pop up from nowhere.

'I don't know what you're on about,' he said, too nonchalantly. 'What moody computer games?'

I rattled off half a dozen Sealsoft games. 'I sell them, sure,' he said defensively. 'But they're not hooky. Look, I got invoices for them,' he added, pushing past me and yanking a drawer open. He pulled out a loose-leaf file and flicked through fast enough to rip a couple of pages before he arrived at a clutch of invoices from Sealsoft.

I took the file from him and walked over to the shelves and counted. 'According to this, Deke, you bought six copies of Sheer Fire II when it was released last month.'

'That's right. And there's only five there now, right? I sold one.'

''Wrong. You sold at least three. That's how many of your customers have returned blank copies of Sheer Fire II to Sealsoft. Care to explain the discrepancy? Or do I have to call your local friendly trading standards officer?' I asked sweetly. 'You can go down for this kind of thing these days, can't you?' I added conversationally.

Half an hour later I was sitting outside Epic PC behind the wheel of Deke's six-year-old Mercedes, waiting for a lad he knew only as Jazbo to turn up in response to a call on his mobile. Amazing what people will do with a little incentive. I spotted Jazbo right away from Deke's description. A shade under six feet, jeans, trainers and a Chicago Cubs bomber jacket. And Tony Blair complains about Manchester United's merchandising.

He got out of a battered boy racer's hatchback clutching a carrier bag with clear, box-shaped outlines pressing against it. I banged off a couple of snaps with the camera in my backpack. Jazbo was in and out of Epic PC inside five minutes. We headed back into town down Bury New Road, me sitting snugly on his tail with only one car between us. We skirted the city centre and headed east. Jazbo eventually parked up in one of the few remaining terraced streets in Gorton and let himself into one of the houses there. I took a note of the address and drove Deke's Merc back to Prestwich before he started getting too twitchy about the idea of me with his wheels.

Next morning I was back outside Jazbo's house just before seven. Early risers, villains, in my experience. According to the electoral roll, Gladys and Albert Conway lived there. I suspected the information on the list was well out of date. With names like that they might have been Jazbo's grandparents, but a more likely scenario was that he'd taken over the house after the Conways had died or suffered the fate worst than death of an old people's home. The man himself emerged about five past the hour. There was less traffic around, but I managed to stay in contact with him into the city centre, where he parked in a loading bay behind Deansgate and let himself into the back of a shop.

I took a chance and left my wheels on a single yellow while I walked round the front of the row of shops and counted back to where Jazbo had let himself in. JJ's Butty Bar. Another piece of the jigsaw clicked into place.

Through the window I caught the occasional glimpse of Jazbo white-coated, moving between tall fridges and worktops. Once or twice he emerged from the rear of the shop with trays of barm cakes neatly wrapped and labelled, and deposited them in the chill cabinets round the shop. I figured he was good for a few hours yet and headed back to the office before the traffic wardens came out to play.

I was back just after two. I kept cruising round the block till someone finally left a meter free that gave me a clear view of the exit from the alley behind the sandwich shop. Jazbo emerged in his hot hatch just after three, which was just as well because I was running out of change. I stayed close to him through the city centre, then let a bit of distance grow between us as he headed out past Salford Quays and into the industrial estate round Trafford Park. He pulled up outside a small unit with Gingerbread House painted in a rainbow of colours across the front wall, and disappeared inside.

About fifteen minutes later he emerged with a supermarket trolley filled to the top with computer-game boxes. I was baffled. I'd had my own theory about where the packaging was coming from, and it had just been blown out of the water. I hate being wrong. I'd rather unblock the toilet. I let Jazbo drive off, then I marched into Gingerbread House. Ten minutes later, I had all the answers.

Fintan O'Donohoe looked impressed as I laid out my dossier before him. Jazbo's address, photograph, phone number, car registration number and place of work would be more than enough to hand him over to the police, gift-wrapped. 'So how's this guy getting hold of the gear?' he demanded.

'First thing I wondered about was the shrink-wrapping. That made me think it was someone in your despatch unit. But you were adamant it couldn't be either your mum or your auntie. Then when I found out he worked in a sandwich shop, I realized he must be using their wrap and seal gear to cover his boxes in. Which left the question of where the boxes were coming from. You ruled out an inside job, so I thought he might simply be raiding your dustbins for discarded gear. But I was wrong. You ever heard of a charity called Gingerbread House?'

O'Donohoe frowned. 'No. Should I have?'

'Your mum has,' I told him. 'And so, I suspect, has Jazbo's mum or girlfriend or sister. Probably took him along to help them carry some gear. It's an educational charity run by some nuns. They go round businesses and ask them for any surplus materials, and they sell them off to schools and playgroups for next to nothing. They collect all sorts - material scraps, bits of bungee rope, offcuts of specialist paper, wallpaper catalogues, tinsel, sheets of plastic, scrap paper. Anything that could come in handy for school projects or for costumes for plays, whatever.'

Fintan O'Donohoe groaned and put his hands over his face. 'Don't tell me . . .'

'They came round here a few months ago, and your mum explained that you don't manufacture here, so there's not much in the way of left-over stuff. But what there was were the boxes from games that had been sent back because they were faulty in some way. The disks were scrapped, and so were the boxes and manuals. If the nuns could make any use of the boxes and their contents . . . They've been dropping them off once a fortnight ever since.'

He looked up at me, a ghost of an ironic smile on his lips. 'And I was so sure it couldn't be anything to do with my mum!'

'Don't they say charity begins at home?'

JOHN OWEN

John Owen has written crime and macabre stories for the magazine market, one of which, 'The Man in the Raincoat', was filmed in the *Alfred Hitchcock Presents* series, and with fellow-Liverpudlian Jim Parkinson has co-authored fifteen radio plays, four (comedies) for the BBC, and the remainder (detective and crime dramas) for German radio. Though both he and Jim write individually, they still collaborate on radio work.

John Owen

MOVIE CRAZY

The 18.10 from Carlisle to Bassett Bridge (alas, no longer running) had a mean speed over the five miles of just twenty-seven miles an hour. Its two coaches were of the old no-corridor variety, divided into compartments with uncomfortable facing seats where eye had tactfully to avoid eye; but as no buses served the route, and the 18.10 was the only evening train, carless commuters to Bassett Bridge held it in high regard.

Tensing at the unexpected whistle - his damned watch must he slow again - Miller broke into his clumsy short-legged run. As he came onto the platform he saw the train beginning to move, and tightening his grip on his paperback, he staggered across the flags, wrenched open a door in the second carriage and flung himself in. He slammed the door shut, dropped into the seat, and was about to curse out his relief when he saw he was not alone.

In the corner diagonally opposite sat a tall, bulky man in a grey chalkstripe suit, a rolled black umbrella laid beside him on the seat. The man's face, though, was at odds with this flagrant respectability, being fleshy, florid and adorned with an immense boozer's nose; he looked, thought Miller wryly, rather like W.C. Fields playing a stockbroker. The man gave him an amiable nod, then returned his attention to the landscape beyond the window.

His pulse settling, Miller's mind began to drift towards thoughts of dinner. He realised he was hungry, and suddenly remembered the packet of peanuts he'd bought from the office vending-machine. He fished it out, tilted it to his mouth and let a few nuts fall onto his tongue. Munching, he took up his book and opened it at the turned-down leaf. 'With *Moby Dick*,' he read, 'John Huston managed to achieve a sympathetic, coherent and intelligent version of a virtually unfilmable novel.' *Not so sure about that*, he thought, and glancing pensively up, saw the stockbroker-Fields figure observing him with an interested smile.

'Sorry,' said Fields, in a voice like brandy trickling over gravel, 'but I couldn't help noticing your book. Talented director, Huston, wasn't he?'

'Yes,' said Miller, 'he was indeed,' and as his companion smiled silently on, he added weakly: 'Extremely, er, versatile.' Fields gazed at him amiably for a second or two longer, nodded, and returned his gaze smoothly to the window.

Hoping that all conversational dues had now been paid, Miller tipped a few more peanuts onto his palm and transferred them to his mouth. He risked another glance at the corner, and saw that Fields was again regarding him with benign interest. It was no good: the bloody man was determined to be sociable, and he'd just have to make the best of it.

'Feeling a bit peckish,' he said, tapping his cheek with a finger. 'I won't be having dinner till seven-thirty, so...' He grinned, and held out the packet. 'Care for some?'

'Kind of you,' said Fields. 'What are they, those Bombay Mix things?'

'No, nuts.'

Fields frowned for a moment, as if considering a matter of supreme importance, then shook his head. 'No, better not, thanks. Got to watch the old waistline, you know.'

'Oh, right,' said Miller brightly; and unable to think of anything to add, he slid the nuts into his pocket and returned to his book. 'Melville's sprawling masterpiece,' he read, 'had previously been filmed in 1930 by Lloyd Bacon, with John Barrymore as a somewhat improbable Ahab.'

'She used to call me that,' said Fields quietly.

Miller looked up. 'Hm?'

'But she doesn't any more,' Fields added, with an amused grunt.

'Sorry? I'm afraid I didn't quite...'

'Look, forgive me for interrupting your reading' - Fields laid his hands on his knees and leaned forward, beaming - 'but I wonder if you'd describe yourself as - what's the phrase - a movie buff?'

'Well... I'm interested in the cinema, yes.'

'Know your stuff, do you?'

'Oh,' Miller shrugged, 'a little bit, I suppose.'

Fields nodded. 'Quite a film fan myself, as a matter of fact. Always have been.'

'Really?' said Miller, trying for an interested air.

'Hm. Wonderful medium, cinema. Always loved it.'

'Ah.' Why, thought Miller, do I always attract bores? 'Well...me too, really.'

'Kindred spirits, eh?' said Fields, and his blue eyes suddenly brightened. 'Wait a minute, I've just had an idea.'

'Oh? What's that?'

'Well, as we're both enthusiasts, and we've got a few minutes to kill' - his grin widened - 'what d'you say to a little quiz?'

'Quiz?'

'Hm. A film quiz.'

'Oh no, I really don't think -

'But why not?' Fields said cheerfully. 'It'll lighten the journey, speed the weary miles!'

'Well,' said Miller, mutely damning all intrusive strangers, 'it's a nice idea, but frankly' - he gave a wry confiding grin - 'I've had a rather bloody sort of day, and...' 'My God, haven't we all,' said Fields. 'Haven't we all. All the more reason to relax a bit, eh? Shrug it all off for a while.'

'Yes, but there wouldn't be time, you see. I'm getting off at the next station.'

'Oh, there'll be time enough for a few quick-fire questions and answers. So how about it, then? What d'you say?'

Miller suddenly found he was too tired to argue. 'All right,' he sighed, 'if you like, but really, I -'

'Good. Splendid.' Fields massaged his large red hands. 'So, a few general knowledge questions on the subject of films. Right, then' - he gave Miller a quick shrewd look, then his smile returned at full wattage - 'get your thinking cap on, because here comes your first question.'

'Oh I see,' said Miller dryly. 'You're asking the questions and I'm answering them, is that it?'

'That's it. Ready?'

'Well - yes, I suppose so.'

'Good. Now then, we're going quite a long way back for this one. Before your time, I should think, but it's a fairly well-known film and you'll probably know it. Name the musical, please, in which the goddess Terpsichore comes down from heaven' - he fluttered his fingers to indicate descent - 'and bestows her love on an ordinary mortal.' He chuckled. 'Well?'

Miller frowned, vaguely hearing the clacking of the wheels over the rail joints. 'Well,' he said, 'I think that'd be - '

'No no, don't *think*,' smiled Fields, 'let's have a positive answer, shall we?'

'All right,' said Miller, slightly ruffled, 'a positive answer, then. *Down to Earth*, made some time in the mid-forties, directed by, er, Alexander Hall.'

'Very good! Right on all counts! And the actress who played Terpsichore?'

'Rita Hayworth.'

'That's right.' Fields' smile had become gentler. 'One of the most beautiful women who ever lived.'

'She certainly was.'

'Yes,' murmured Fields. 'I used to be crazy about that woman. Absolutely crazy.' He shook his head briskly, as if to clear it of the vapours of nostalgia. 'Well, you certainly seem to know your movies.'

'Oh, well, I think I was just lucky with that one -'

'So I think we might make it a wee bit more challenging for you,' Fields beamed, 'if we put a time limit on the answers.'

'Time limit?' Miller winced. 'Look, don't you think that's taking it a bit too -'

'Ten seconds,' said Fields genially. 'All right?'

Miller shrugged, found himself outfaced by the man's brilliant smile and glanced out of the window. Trees, a grassy hillock, another clump of trees moved swiftly past. The train always made good time along this particular stretch, and its rocking motion was beginning to make him uneasy; which was odd, because it had never bothered him before.

'Right,' came the gravelly voice, 'question number two.'

He refocused on Fields, and for the first time noticed the man's eyes: there was something distinctly odd about them, a sort of cold hard glee...

'Name the early German sound film in which a respectable schoolmaster marries a heartless trollop' - Fields' grin faltered for a moment - 'who destroys his life and finally drives him mad.' A nerve twitched in his left cheek. 'One. Two. Three...'

'*The Blue Angel*,' said Miller quickly. 'Emil Jannings and Marlene Dietrich. Nineteen-thirty.'

'Absolutely right,' said Fields, chuckling. 'Full marks.'

'Remade,' Miller added, feeling a sudden need to please, 'in nineteen fifty-nine.'

However, he seemed to have touched the wrong button, for Fields' smile had suddenly faded. 'That's right,' he murmured, 'they remade it. Hell of a mess they made of it, though, didn't they? Tried to give the woman a heart. Which made nonsense of the whole damn thing, of course, because the bitch didn't have one. She was completely without feeling.' The nerve twitched. 'Cold. Callous. Ruthless.'

'Yes,' said Miller, nodding earnestly, 'yes, the remake was a bit of a travesty, really.'

'Complete bloody travesty,' said Fields grimly. 'Anyway,' he continued, the smile flashing on again, 'you're doing very well so far, so here comes question number three. Now then, tell me this, please, and don't forget the time-limit. In the film *Night of the Hunter*, what weapon did Robert Mitchum use to, er, dispatch Shelley Winters?' His eyes twinkled roguishly. 'One...'

'Well,' Miller stammered, 'Mitchum played a preacher, and, ah-'

'Four, that's not what I asked you, five - '

'Wait a minute, I know it, he killed her with, ah - '

'Eight, nine-'

'*With a knife!*'

'Quite correct,' said Fields serenely. 'With a knife. Quick, clean and simple.' His smile became mischievous, and he wagged a finger at Miller. 'Just got that one in time, didn't you?'

'Yes, ha ha.'

'Just dodged the penalty.'

'Penalty?' Miller gave a quick violent wriggle. 'This is new. What sort of, er, penalty's that, then?'

Fields leaned forward, rested his lobster-pink hands on his knees and grinned like a naughty boy. He spoke softly against a rapidly-rising noise, and his lips had formed two inaudible words that looked alarmingly like 'The supreme' when the compartment, as if on cue, was swallowed in a roaring melodramatic darkness.

'Sorry?' Miller peered stupidly at the corner, but the darkness was absolute, even the man's eyes had been extinguished and he might be anywhere now, he might have sneaked across to Miller's side and be edging along the seat towards him...

The clatter died, sunlight exploded into the compartment and Fields was still safely in his corner, poised on the seat's edge, smiling his unvarying smile.

'You know,' said Miller brightly, his fingers moistly intertwined, 'it sounds absurd, but for a moment I thought you said - '

'Right!' Fields clapped his hands on his knees. 'Wits honed, brain fully engaged, ready for question number four?'

'Oh yes, absolutely.'

'Good. Here we go, then. In Hitchcock's marvellous thriller *Rear Window*, how did the husband smuggle his wife's body out of the apartment without anyone knowing?' His eyebrows lifted in jovial enquiry. 'One, two...'

'Ah yes, I know that one, wait a minute.'

'Three, four - '

'Hang on - '

'Five, six - '

'He smuggled her out, er - '

'Seven - '

'In pieces! Yes! In tiny little pieces! Wrapped up in parcels!'

'Quite correct,' said Fields, beaming approval. 'Yes, that's how it was done. Clever, eh?'

'Oh yes. Very, er, ingenious.'

'Had 'em all completely baffled, ha ha.'

'Yes,' said Miller, his sudden high-pitched giggle surprising himself, 'I know.'

Fields' smiled snapped off like a light. 'You know?' he said quietly.

Miller stared helplessly into the wintry blue eyes, made a couple of false starts and then said hoarsely, 'Well, yes - I saw the picture, of course.'

'Ah.' A series of small nervous impulses, starting with a twitch of the huge nose and extending to the cheeks, seemed to find an outlet in the muscles of Fields' mouth, which finally lifted in a smile. 'The picture. Yes of course.' He chuckled. 'Anyway, that's that one out of the way, and it brings us on rather neatly, I think, to your last little teaser.'

'Thank God,' said Miller unthinkingly.

'Ah yes' - Fields raised an admonitive finger - 'but you haven't actually answered it yet, have you?'

'Well, no, ha ha.'

'So let's just see how you get on, shall we? And of course being the final question, it's going to be just a *wee* bit more difficult. Now then, listen carefully. Name the film, please, in which Donald Pleasance utters the immortal line: "They can't prove a thing without her body, and her body's scattered over two lakes, three rivers and a millpond." Your time,' he added genially, 'starts now.'

'Millpond, eh.' Miller gave a tight little smile. 'Donald Pleasence. Well now.'

'One.'

'D'you know,' said Miller, 'I'm afraid I don't - '

'Two.'

'I'm afraid I don't know it.'

'Three.'

'Look - any chance of a clue?'

'Four,' said Fields, still as stone except for his lips.

'A hint, even. Just a little hint.'

'Five.'

'A little help! Please!'

'Six.'

'Help!'

'Seven.'

Miller glanced at the hedges whizzing beyond the window. He could fling himself out and risk a broken neck, or stay where he was and -

'Eight,' said the smiling statue.

The communication cord wasn't any use either, because the train would take some seconds to stop, and by then -

'Nine.'

Tiny blue stars were exploding about his head. 'No,' he groaned, 'it's no good, I - '

'Ten,' said Fields, and got to his feet with astonishing swiftness.

'I don't know it!' Miller yelled, wedging himself into the corner, 'I just don't bloody know it!'

'No,' murmured Fields, advancing 'I'm afraid you don't, do you?'

Miller grabbed his paperback and held it before him like a pigmy shield. 'Get back!'

'Sorry, old chap,' said Fields, smiling down with what almost seemed sincere regret, 'but it's penalty time.' He lifted his hands and stared at them for a moment, flexing his fingers.

'Listen,' said Miller, 'you need help, you're not well - '

'These hands,' said Fields reflectively, 'are immensely strong. Immensely.'

'Listen! Please!'

'You'll find,' crooned Fields, extending his hands smoothly towards Miller's throat, 'that this'll hardly hurt at all. Goodbye, old man.'

'Get away from me, you maniac!' Miller flailed vainly at him with his book. 'You're crazy, d'you know that? You're gaga! You're completely bloody...'

He choked, as the fingers began to tighten. 'Nuts!' he croaked despairingly.

Fields blinked, and his expression of smiling intensity suddenly softened. A slight frown gathered on his forehead; his hands dropped to his sides, and for a few moments he stood gently swaying to the train's motion, making small jerky movements with his head as if to dismiss a persistent insect.

'Ah, no thanks,' he said vaguely. 'Got to watch the old waistline, you know.'

He turned, lowered himself gently to the seat opposite Miller and fell back against the headrest. 'My God,' he murmured, passing a hand across his brow, 'I feel as if I've been on a three-day binge.' He gave Miller a quick, faintly embarrassed look. 'Did I snore, by the way?'

Miller stared inanely. 'Snore?' he whispered, after a second or two.

'Hm. Sorry if I did. I'm afraid I usually do, even when it's only forty winks.'

'No,' said Miller, gently touching a forefinger and thumb to his throat. 'No, you didn't snore.'

'Ah, well that's something, anyway. I know how annoying it can be.' His polite smile faltered. 'Er, look, old man, I don't want to seem nosy, but are you feeling quite well? You look just a little bit - '

'No, I'm fine,' Miller said quickly. 'Fine, really.' A sudden scream stabbed into his head like migraine, persisting horribly; for a split-second he wondered if it was coming from his own throat, then recognised it as the sound of the train braking.

The platform slid into view, a grizzled porter in a shabby uniform, an old lady clutching the hand of a fat little girl. The train gave a series of small jolts and came to a halt, shivering slightly.

He got up, heaved at the door and finally managed to wrench it open. 'Your book, sir,' came Fields' voice amiably; 'your John Huston.' Miller grabbed the paperback from the seat, bobbed his head to Fields and stumbled out.

'Cheerio,' said Fields from within.

Miller gave a weak little wave and slammed the door shut; from behind the glass, the rosy face inclined in a courteous farewell. A whistle blew, the train shuddered, and glass and face moved smoothly away together.

Miller stared after the train until it dwindled into a toy, then turned and walked with small careful steps towards the ticket-office. The old lady eyed him with flinty disapproval, the fat little girl gazed solemnly, the porter's grin was wry with derision, and he suddenly realised that he was giggling to himself, fatuously, like some clownish early-evening drunk.

JIM PARKINSON

Jim Parkinson has spent most of his life in the Book Trade initially as a bookseller and, latterly, as a publisher of Local History. From short stories he progressed to writing Radio Drama (some comedy, mostly crime) in collaboration with fellow CWA member John Owen and has recently completed his first novel. He lives with his wife and daughter in Liverpool.

Jim Parkinson

DOUBLE EXPOSURE

Alec Denny had just poured himself a second cup of coffee when his wife, Maeve, brought up the subject of shoes.

'....just right for my Jersey-wool dress. Fitted perfectly, too. The woman said she could hold them for a couple of days but that's all.'

Mindful of the well-stocked wardrobes upstairs, Alec frowned and said, 'I thought you had plenty of shoes.'

'Well, I have but it's just that these are...' Maeve hesitated and a shadow fell across her face. 'No, you're right, Alec, I don't really need them. I'm sorry. I shouldn't have mentioned it.'

Alec sipped his coffee and sighed. 'How much are they?'

Maeve glanced up at him eagerly. 'They've been reduced. They're only forty pounds.'

Alec, who had never spent forty pounds on a pair of shoes in his life, sighed again. 'Look, love, it isn't that I don't want you to have them...' The disappointment in his wife's eyes forced an explanation from him. 'It's just that - well - things are a bit tight at the moment.'

He was speaking no more than the truth. Denny Investigations, like many other small businesses in a Liverpool that was only slowly emerging from the recession, was going through something of a bad patch. On his own he could have accepted the reduction in his income and adapted his life-style accordingly but his marriage, two years ago, to Maeve had placed an increasingly intolerable strain on his financial resources. From the very first, she had seemed to regard him as some sort of cornucopia... an endless source of new clothes, jewellery and expensive cosmetics.

Initially, infatuated with her as he was, he hadn't minded. Her pleasure had given him pleasure. But, as the colour of his bank statements had turned from black to red and the communications from his bank manager had become more frequent and less civil, he had tried, without noticeable success, to curb her extravagance.

Maeve's voice broke into his thoughts. 'It doesn't matter, Alec, really. I can manage without them.' She stood up, walked round the breakfast table and kissed the top of his head. 'I know you'd let me have them if you could.'

Alec leant his head against her breast and felt the old familiar weakness steal over him. 'Let me think about it. If it's possible...'

She ruffled his hair and returned to her seat. Alec drained his cup and stood up. 'Anyway, I'd better get a move on. I've got Ellison coming in at ten o'clock.'

'Ellison?'

'The chap from Northern and Provincial. It could be very important.' He waited briefly for a response but his wife had already turned to the pages of a fashion catalogue that had arrived in the morning post. 'She's a child,' he thought resignedly, 'a beautiful, spoilt child.' He walked down the hallway and let himself out into the warm summer sunshine. His elderly Volvo started at the first touch and he joined the stream of traffic taking the riverside route into town.

Opposite the Albert Dock he turned right, skirted Chinatown with its crouched green lions and bi-lingual street signs and, arriving at the top of the hill, parked his car in Gambier Terrace. Locking the car he stood for a moment savouring the view. In front of him the vast sandstone bulk of the Anglican Cathedral was framed by the glittering waters of the Mersey. Beyond were the gentle undulations of the Wirral and, farther off still, just discernible through the morning haze, the blue whalebacks of the Welsh hills.

Normally it was a prospect that raised Alec's spirits but this morning he had more pressing matters on his mind. During the short walk to his office his thoughts returned again to the significance of this morning's meeting with Ellison.

The regular and lucrative work the insurance company could put his way would make all the difference to Denny Investigations. He was in with a chance, he knew, but he wasn't the only one in the running and... He was halfway up the narrow flight of stairs leading to his first-floor office when he heard the shrill sound of his telephone and broke into a run. Swiftly unlocking his office door he hurled himself across the room and snatched up the receiver.

'Denny Investigations!'

'Alec, old son!'

Alec sat down before speaking. The sprint upstairs had left him slightly out of breath.

'Leo. What can I do for you?'

Leo's voice, an eclectic mixture of North Country, Surrey Golf Club and Hollywood B Movie was, as ever, relentlessly cheerful. 'What you can do is haul your backside round here pronto. I've got another job for you.'

Alec groaned. He could have done without this today of all days. 'Sorry, Leo, I can't manage this morning. I'll try and slip round later on. After lunch.'

He heard Leo snigger at the other end of the line.

'Just wait till you see this one...an absolute dish. Wouldn't mind a crack at her myself.'

'Yes, well...as I say, I'll see you later.'

Alec replaced the receiver, pushed his chair back and put his feet up on the desk. Leo's call had depressed him...was it his imagination or had the sunlight streaming in at the window behind him suddenly become less intense? Leo was a problem, there was no doubt about it, and it was a thousand pities he had ever got mixed up with him in the first place.

He brightened as a thought occurred to him. If his forthcoming interview was a success and Northern and Provincial took him on board then he could kiss goodbye to Leo and their unsavoury relationship for ever. Cheered by this thought and by Ellison's imminent arrival Alec stirred himself into action.

He spent the next few minutes clearing his desk of files, emptying ashtrays and carrying dirty coffee mugs through to the cubby-hole that served as his kitchen and when, shortly after ten o'clock, he opened the door to Ellison he was satisfied that, for once, his office presented an image of organised efficiency.

An hour and a half later Alec shook Ellison warmly by the hand and closed the door behind him. As he heard his visitor's footsteps recede into silence on the stairwell he punched the air and mouthed a triumphant, if muted, 'Yes!' The interview had gone exactly as he'd hoped it would. The contract was signed and, for the first time in many months, Alec felt that there was light at the end of his financial tunnel.

Suddenly, he felt the urge to share his good news. But with whom? No point in ringing Maeve - she'd probably be out somewhere and, even if he did catch her at home, he was unlikely to get the required response from her. 'Robbie! Of course!' Alec lifted the receiver and tapped in the number of the car show-room owned by his best friend Robbie Briers. He was quickly put through by the receptionist and smiled as he heard his old chum's welcoming and breezy tones, 'Alec, good to hear from you...'

Pleasantries over, Alec launched into an account of his recent good fortune. Robbie, as he had known he would be, was genuinely delighted.

'Alec, that's terrific. You deserve it...and it couldn't have happened to a nicer guy. We must...ah, hang on a minute, will you?' There was the sound of a murmured conversation at the other end of the line before Robbie spoke again. 'Sorry, Alec, but I'm afraid I have to go...something's just come up. Look, why don't you and Maeve come over for a bite to eat on Saturday? It's ages since the four of us got together.'

Alec readily agreed to the suggestion and arrangements were quickly made. 'It'll be good to see them again,' he thought as he replaced the receiver. Robbie and Jo were so obviously the ideal couple. Even their constant teasing was, he knew, their way of saying how much they loved each other.

He glanced at his watch. Almost twelve...a little early for lunch. 'But then again,' he thought with a satisfied grin, 'perhaps a small celebration might be in order.' He switched on his answering machine and let himself out of the office.

An hour later, fortified by a couple of pints of The Mitre's excellent beer, Alec left the city-centre pub and turned in the direction of Leo's photographic studio. He used the ten-minute walk to consider carefully what he was going to say to Leo. It wasn't easy.

Leo Thompson was more of an acquaintance of Alec's than a friend although recently they had become partners of a kind in a new business enterprise. They had first met in the Caernarvon Castle where they were both in the habit of taking a liquid lunch. Initially, he had been attracted to Leo's outgoing and expansive personality. It was only recently that he had discovered another, darker, side to the man's nature.

Their present collaboration had begun some months ago when, over beer and sandwiches, he had told the photographer about the case he was currently working on. It was the sort of assignment that came Alec's way occasionally - a jealous husband had hired him to follow his wife who, he suspected, was seeing another man. At lunchtime the previous day Alec had followed the woman and her boyfriend (the husband's suspicions proving to be fully justified) to a car-park in Howarth Forest, a National Trust property a few miles north of Liverpool. Cast reluctantly in the role of voyeur, and from behind the cover of a convenient tree, Alec had observed the couple engaged in 'a bit of nooky' (Leo's phraseology, not his own). So far, so good, but what had astonished Alec was the amount of similar activity going on in other cars dotted about the remoter corners of the car-park.

'There must have been half-a-dozen couples at it, Leo. In broad daylight. I could hardly believe what I was seeing. I mean, haven't they got homes to do that sort of thing in?'

Leo had taken a long swallow of his beer before replying. 'You're missing the point, Alec, old lad. I'll bet you another pint those couples you saw weren't married...at least, not to each other.' He smirked knowingly. 'Let's face it, if you wanted to have it away with your secretary at lunchtime, where better to go than Howarth Forest?'

Alec reluctantly conceded that Leo was probably right but then the conversation had moved on and he had forgotten all about the matter when, a couple of days later, Leo had asked him for a favour. They were seated at their usual table in the Caernarvon Castle when Leo pushed a scrap of paper across to Alec on which was written the registration number of a car.

'You've got a contact, haven't you, Alec? Someone who can put a name and address to this number?'

Alec nodded. He did have a contact in police records who, for a consideration, would perform such a service. It was a service which had proved useful in the past but one that he was reluctant to use too often.

'Why d'you ask?'

Leo put his forefinger to the side of his nose. 'Can't tell you that. But I want this character's name and address...job, likely income, marital status...that sort of thing.'

Alec was about to demur but Leo forestalled him by pushing an envelope across the table. 'There's two hundred and fifty quid in there, Alec. That's for your expenses and for not asking any questions. All right?'

Alec hesitated but the offer had come just a few hours after his latest catastrophic bank statement. He picked up the envelope and slipped it into his pocket. 'I'll see what I can do,' he promised.

He had been puzzled by Leo's request but had done what had been asked of him. When he had dropped the required information off with the photographer two days later Leo was pleased but no more forthcoming than before.

Early the following week Leo had invited him around to the studio to ask him for another 'favour'. Again there were two hundred and fifty pounds in an envelope but this time Alec demanded answers. 'I'll do it, Leo, but I want to know what's going on. That's the deal.'

The plump, untidily-dressed man opposite him thought for a moment then, apparently coming to a decision, crossed to a filing cabinet from which he took a large manilla envelope. Returning to the desk he sat down and, taking from the envelope a sheaf of photographs, handed them to Alec. 'That's what it's about,' he said.

Alec looked at the photographs which, in their clarity, were a tribute to Leo's professional skill. They showed, in astonishingly explicit detail, a man and woman making love in the back seat of a car. As he flicked through the photographs he could see both of the participant's faces clearly and, behind the car, a background of trees and bushes which he quickly recognised as Howarth Forest. The last photograph was a close-up of the car's registration number...the same number that Leo had given him a couple of minutes earlier.

Alec was accustomed to thinking of himself as a man of the world - the nature of his work had left him with few illusions about his fellow man - but it was several seconds before he was fully able to comprehend the significance of what he was holding in his hand. He looked across the desk at his smiling companion.

'Blackmail!' he said incredulously. 'You're blackmailing them.'

Leo's smile broadened as he nodded his agreement. 'Spot on, Alec. And highly profitable it's going to be - already is - for both of us.'

Alec pushed the photographs back across the desk. 'Sorry, Leo, you've got the wrong man. I may have sailed pretty close to the wind in my time but blackmail...that's something else.'

Leo leaned forward. 'You gave me the idea, Alec. You told me what went on up there and when I took a little run that way I discovered that everything you said was true.'

'But that's no reason...'

Leo held up his hand. 'Spare me the sermon, Alec. There's no need to feel sorry for them, you know. I only pick on the ones who can afford it...the fat cats in their big cars. Face it, these are men who are ratting on their wives and families. They're having their bit on the side...it's only reasonable that they should pay for it.'

Thinking about it later Alec had tried, without success, to recall the ensuing conversation. Certainly Leo had been an eloquent and persuasive advocate and he had caught Alec at a moment when his financial problems were rapidly assuming the proportions of a nightmare. Nonetheless, he was still baffled (and ashamed) at how easily he had succumbed to the photographer's blandishments.

That conversation had taken place several months earlier and since then Alec had passed on the details of six or seven 'marks' receiving in return the same number of brown envelopes stuffed with crisp, consoling ten-pound notes. What Leo did with this information - how he went about the actual mechanics of blackmail - Alec had no idea and hadn't sought enlightenment. He suspected that Leo was making a great deal more from the operation than he was and conceded the fairness of that. And there was no denying it, he thought as he turned the corner and arrived in front of Leo's studio, the money he had so far received had gone a long way towards reducing his overdraft.

He pushed the door open and went in. The morose-looking girl behind the counter who was busily, if not usefully, engaged in filing her nails looked up at Alec's entrance and inclined her head in the direction of a door at the rear of the studio.

''E's in the office.'

Alec nodded his thanks, crossed to the door and went in. The room - Leo's office - was an accurate reflection of the man himself...large, untidy and permanently reeking of tobacco smoke. In front of the room's only window stood a desk the top of which was disfigured by coffee-rings and the scorch- marks of innumerable cigars. Behind this desk sat Leo, inevitable cigar in mouth and radiating bonhomie and self-satisfaction in equal measure.

'Alec, old lad! Glad you could make it.' He indicated a seat facing him. 'Park it there.'

Alec parked it. His good humour of the past hour or so had evaporated during the short walk from The Mitre to Leo's studio. He loathed this room, he loathed Leo and, above all, he loathed himself for being there and for what Leo had turned him into.

His face must have mirrored his distaste because Leo grinned and said, 'Cheer up, Alec. It might never happen.'

Alec grunted. 'It won't happen again, Leo. This is the last one...I mean it.'

Leo cocked his head to one side, his whole attitude evincing disbelief. 'All right, old son, whatever you say. You're the boss.'

He winked and drew from his pocket an envelope. 'It's all there. No need to count it.'

He lobbed the envelope to Alec who caught it and thrust it into the inside pocket of his jacket. He had no intention of counting the money. At least not here...he wouldn't give Leo that satisfaction.

'Right, let's have a look at them, then.'

Leo's grin broadened. He opened a drawer in his desk and took out one of the now-familiar manilla envelopes which he skimmed across the desk to Alec. As usual there was a car registration number written in ink on the top corner.

'This guy should be loaded. Latest model BMW with a personalised number plate. Always a good sign, that.'

Alec glanced idly at the number then stiffened with shock.

ROB 1!

He stared at the number in disbelief.

From a great distance he heard Leo say, 'Handle them with care, Alec, they're red hot.'

Alec hesitated before slowly easing open the envelope and taking out the sheaf of photographs. Their quality was well up to Leo's highest professional standards...every detail crystal clear. There could be no possible mistake or alternative explanation. The man in the photographs was his best friend, Robbie Briers.

It was after seven o'clock when Alec's Volvo drew to a halt outside his house. He let himself in and walked through into the living room where he found Maeve watching an early-evening soap on the television. She jumped up as he came into the room, crossed to him and kissed him. 'Alec, you're late. I was getting worried about you.'

He detached himself from her embrace and threw himself into an armchair.

'Sorry, love, it's been a busy day. Lots to tell you.'

She looked at him enquiringly.

'First, those shoes you were telling me about this morning...'

'What about them?'

'Well, if they're as nice as you say they are I think you should have them.'

Maeve's face lit up just as he had known it would and she came and perched on the arm of his chair. 'Alec, you are a darling. I don't deserve you, I don't really.'

Alec smiled and squeezed her hand. 'And there's something else. I got that contract with Northern and Provincial. It's going to make a big difference to us so, tonight, I thought we should push the boat out a bit. I've booked us a table at the Lighthouse.'

Maeve's eyes opened wide. 'Oh, Alec, how lovely!'

The Lighthouse, with its cliff-top views across the Dee estuary to the Welsh coast, was her favourite restaurant. It was expensive but the food was always good and it boasted just the sort of romantic ambience which she most enjoyed. In their courting days the two of them had often dined there although it had been many months now since their last visit.

'Well, it's such a fine evening,' Alec said. 'And after dinner I thought we might go for a stroll along the headland...like we used to.'

Maeve pursed her lips and looked at him archly. 'So, that's your little game, is it? Well, we'll have to see how it goes, won't we?'

The reference to Alec's 'little game,' as they both knew, was to a similarly balmy evening before they were married when, carried away by the wine they had drunk and the moonlit beauty of the cliff-top, they had made love for the first time in a heather-filled hollow. Maeve moved towards the door.

'You have a drink and relax while I get changed. I won't be long.' She threw him a smile and left the room.

Alec heaved himself out of his chair, crossed to the drinks-tray and poured himself a whisky. 'Perhaps I shouldn't be doing this,' he thought as he sipped it slowly. He certainly mustn't drink too much at the restaurant. Apart from the risk of losing his driving licence the cliff-top path, safe enough in daylight, wasn't a place to wander along after dark if you were a bit unsteady on your legs. In two or three places it came within head-spinning proximity of the cliff-edge with its hundred foot drop to the rocks below. One false step or alcohol-induced stumble and... He shuddered at the thought and walked out into the hall.

'Maeve!' He could hear her moving about in the bedroom above then, a moment later, she was at the bannister, her lustrous mane of red hair hanging forward and partly concealing the pale skin of her face as she leaned over to look at him.

'What is it?'

'Would you do something for me?'

'What?'

There was a constriction in Alec's throat that made it difficult for him to articulate the words. 'Would you wear my favourite dress?' Maeve looked puzzled. 'The silk one with the green and white stripes. I always think it makes you look very sexy.'

His wife smiled and shook her head in mock exasperation. 'Alec, we're a respectable married couple...'

'But you'll wear it?'

'Yes, if you like.' She smiled again and disappeared from his sight.

Alec walked back into the living-room, sat down and picked up his drink. He was breathing hard and noticed that his hand holding the glass was trembling. He closed his eyes and rested his head on the back of the chair and, as he did so, a series of images came into his mind - images he had been striving to hold at bay since his visit to Leo's that afternoon.

The first was of Leo himself, the cigar in his mouth failing to mask the leer on his face as he tossed the envelope containing the photographs across his desk. After a moment this picture lost shape, fragmented and then re-defined itself. Now Alec was looking at the first of the photographs which showed Robbie and a woman in a car. The woman was several years younger than Robbie, pale-skinned and with a tumbling mass of red hair. The image changed again. In the next photograph the couple were locked in a passionate embrace, Robbie's hand fumbling urgently at the buttons of the woman's dress...a low-cut dress of some kind of silky material...a dress patterned vividly in green and white stripes...!

Abruptly, Alec started forward in his chair, opened his eyes and gazed unseeingly before him. His forehead was damp with perspiration and somewhere at the back of his skull a pulse had begun to beat insistently...remorselessly...

NICHOLAS RHEA

(Photo: Jozef)

NICHOLAS RHEA was a police officer for 30 years. His duties included press relations and lecturing in criminal law. Author of about 100 books, he won the *Police Review* Award for *Murder after the Holiday*, while his *Constable* titles featuring a 1960's constable on the North York Moors were adapted for the TV series, *Heartbeat*. He is a past-chairman of the Crime Writers Association, President of Nottingham Writers Club, and a member of the Mystery Writers of America.

Nicholas Rhea is the pen-name of Peter N. Walker

Nicholas Rhea

A CASE OF CHRISTMAS SPIRIT

The trumpeting of a fractured exhaust pipe heralded the arrival of Glenys Hutchinson at Aidensfield Stores. Amid a salvo of bangs and blasts the rusty, mud-spattered Morris Traveller halted before me. Anyone else with a faulty exhaust would avoid the village constable - but not Glenys. Cheerful as always, she disarmed me with a smile.

"I'm in a rush, constable, and I know what you're going to say. I just haven't had time to get it fixed...I'll get a replacement from Claude Jeremiah, then I want a word about the Christmas party, so don't go away..."

And with that, Glenys disappeared into the shop. In her mid-thirties with delightful elfin features, she had striking white teeth, short dark hair and dark eyes with a hint of freckles about her nose. Her slender, attractive body was now broadening as she approached middle age but she didn't seem to care. She rushed about in old clothes too - she was as poor as the proverbial church mouse yet always found the time and energy to do things for others.

The moorland smallholding she ran with her husband barely produced a living wage which explained their poverty and grotty car. It was invariably parked in the village as she went about her self-imposed tasks. Unfortunately, there was usually something wrong with it. That was not surprising because it carried everything from cattle food to live poultry.

That meant the interior was as mucky as the exterior but that didn't worry Glenys either. Alec's constant struggle to earn a living meant he rarely had time for outings, so it was Glenys who sallied forth with piglets in the back or eggs on the floor. Many trips resulted in rusty bits dropping off or strange noises among the moving parts. Neither had money to lavish on their decaying vehicle nor had they spare cash to spend on new clothes in spite of striving ceaselessly on their miniature ranch. Few could remember the last time Glenys had her hair done or bought herself a new dress but in spite of her poverty, she was never gloomy. She went cheerfully about life in the most robust manner.

I was acquainted with Glenys because of that faulty vehicle - either the exhaust was hanging loose, a mudguard was flapping, the number plate was illegible or light bulbs had blown and I had to tell her to correct the defects. If Sergeant Blaketon noticed them, she'd be in trouble - and so would I! To be fair, she or Alec did obtain second-hand replacements from Claude Jeremiah Greengrass, although I did wonder where Claude found his supplies; some were in very good condition. In spite of it all, I never took the Hutchinsons to court - village bobbies didn't do that sort of thing. A word at the right time was sufficient.

Lately, though, Glenys had become forgetful. She began to leave her car doors unlocked with the key in the ignition. I'd often warned her it was an invitation to thieves, even in the moorland calm of Aidensfield, but she'd said "Nobody steals cars in Aidensfield, Constable Nick!"

"There's always a first time," was my standard retort, whereupon she would merely smile and thank me - then promptly do it again. She existed in a permanent whirl of activity and I wondered if she and Alec ever experienced moments of calm with one another. Although their work on the smallholding was so time-consuming, Glenys helped the old folks with shopping, sometimes giving them eggs or vegetables she could ill-afford; she lit their fires in winter or cooked their meals, but in addition, always ran the annual Christmas Party in Aidensfield village hall.

In this case, she did persuade others to help with the food or Christmas presents. Claude Jeremiah Greengrass always played Father Christmas and I helped with the decorations and Christmas tree. Lots of people had a job but it was Glenys who made things happen. As Christmas approached, she raced around with her old Morris full of Christmassy things instead of hens or piglets - and that's what she was doing now. This year's party was fast approaching and she seemed more cheerful and lively than usual.

I went to peer into her car and sure enough, she'd left the keys in the ignition! As I sighed in exasperation, Edna Pryer appeared behind me. She was the 50-year old purveyor of Aidensfield gossip and had also noticed the noisy arrival of Glenys.

"You should do something about that noise, Constable! And I say it's a pity Glenys Hutchinson hasn't a family to keep her at home! That's what I say. Rushing about like she does..."

"She does a lot of good work," I countered. "Some old folks rely on her."

"She ought to spend more time with that husband of hers, then she might produce a family. I'm not surprised she hasn't children, all that gallivanting about..."

"Really?" I had no intention of fuelling Edna's gossip.

"There's no secrets in a place like this - you ought to know! They've had all the tests and they're both all right. Too much rushing about, that's what I say."

"Those old people and children, they're her family," I spoke in defence of Glenys. "If she can't have children herself, it explains all her good work for others."

"She's as busy as a wasp in a jam jar, it's time she settled down, Constable," and Edna stomped away, having imparted her vision of the ideal world.

If Glenys couldn't have a child, it might explain her activities. She loved people; she needed them and gave them lots of her time, with gifts too - useful things like food. As Edna left me, Glenys emerged with her arms full of groceries. She placed them in her car, then turned to go back into the shop.

"I'd forget my head if it was loose!" she laughed as she rushed away. "Mr Stead's out of tea, Miss Browne needs more washing powder and my Alec's run out of toothpaste...you won't forget the meeting tomorrow, will you, Nick? About the Christmas party."

"No," I assured her. "I won't. And you weren't going to leave those keys in the ignition, were you?"

She issued a massive sigh and laughed. "I'll only be a minute ...keep an eye on it for me, will you?"

And so I stood guard upon the muddy old Traveller - and noticed its tax disc expired at the end of December. I'd have to remind her to renew it.

The Aidensfield Christmas party was on the Tuesday before Christmas and comprised an afternoon session for children with Father Christmas, games and food. This was followed by an evening period for older adults with presents for pensioners, a supper and old-time dancing. It ended with more dancing to pop music for the younger element. Glenys had persuaded old Mrs Habton to wrap the presents and put names on them; they'd be ready for collection on the morning of the party. When I was chatting to Mrs Habton, she told me, "I did enjoy doing the parcels but I had no idea Mr Greengrass was a pensioner!"

"Neither had I!" I had to admit. "He's kept that very quiet!"

"The Post Office told me," grinned Mrs Habton. "He sneaks in to draw his pension but if anybody's there, he pretends he's shopping...he's very secretive about his age, you know..."

"Really?" I commented, wondering why Claude wished to conceal his advancing years.

But as party day approached, there were more important things than Claude Jeremiah's age to worry about. Glenys told me she'd bought a splendid replacement exhaust from Claude and announced she would collect Mrs Habton's parcels and deliver them to the hall, at the same time collecting the cooked turkeys from the butcher, some bread rolls from the baker, bottles of orange juice and lemonade from the Co-op and the specially baked Christmas cake from Mrs Cooper of Elsinby. There was a box of spirits to collect from the Off-Licence in Ashfordly too - bottles of gin, whisky and brandy which were raffle prizes.

But this year, there was a secret and very pleasant job to do. Chairman of the Parish Council, Stanley Preston, had approached committee members to suggest,

"Glenys does all this with no thought of a reward in spite of being so short of money, so how about a surprise presentation to her at the party?"

Everyone had agreed but some had asked, "What on earth shall we get her?"

"She could do with some new clothes, a nice dress or suit, shoes, something special," was the general consensus among the ladies. "She's desperately hard up."

"What about a gift voucher, then she could get what she wants," was another idea. "She might be insulted if we restrict it to clothes."

It was decided there would be a cash collection to provide an open gift voucher for Glenys. She could treat herself to whatever she wanted, the proviso being that the gift would be for her, and her alone, not to be given to any of the villagers. As the days grew colder and the darkening nights carried a threat of snow on the moors, I got the job of making the collection. I managed to raise £46. 10s. 6d, a very useful sum when a weekly wage was around £12.

I knew that Alec and Glenys existed on much less - the voucher would be a wonderful present. Somehow, the villagers managed to keep the secret from Glenys, then on the morning before the party, as I was patrolling on my motor bike, a few isolated snowflakes floated from the grey clouds.

I was concerned that snow was forecast and hoped it wouldn't hinder the party arrangements. That morning, Glenys collected the presents so carefully wrapped and labelled by Mrs Habton, along with other party items. Placing everything in her car, she drove into Ashfordly to collect the spirits from the Off-Licence and decided to do some last minute shopping of her own. She needed a Christmas card for Alec, and all he wanted as a present was a new pair of corduroys, if she could afford them. Glenys had saved up and there was just time to buy the cords before returning to Aidensfield - and the snow held off but the sky remained grey and threatening.

In Ashfordly, Glenys had collected the spirits and placed the bottles in her car before walking to the stationers. She hadn't noticed two youths watching her and by the time she emerged with Alec's card, her car had gone. At first, she didn't believe it. She searched the street, the car park, the side streets...but the Traveller wasn't there. It took several minutes to realise it had been stolen, along with all the food, the presents, the drinks and extra items for Aidensfield's Christmas party.

Devastated, Glenys just stood on the pavement and wept.

By chance, I was on my way to Ashfordly Police Station and saw the unhappy figure sobbing in the street. I parked the motor bike and went to her.

"Glenys?"

"Oh, Nick...thank God it's you...it's awful...I'm so ashamed...it's ruined, everything's ruined.."

"What's ruined? What's happened?"

"You're going to be very angry....you warned me..." she sobbed. "My car's gone, stolen. It was right here...it's got all the party stuff inside as well, it's all gone, every bit of it. All that work, all for nothing..."

This was the latest in a long spate of similar car thefts but I didn't ask if she'd left the keys in the ignition. Her eyes moist with tears, she pleaded. "What can I do? It's all my fault...all those children will be waiting...."

I put a comforting arm around her shoulders and said, "Come on, the police station's just around the corner. We'll circulate details, it can't be far away."

Sergeant Blaketon confirmed that several cars had been stolen in recent months and not recovered. They'd contained handbags, cameras and things of similar value but those taken in the last few days had contained either cigarettes or spirits, so popular with thieves at Christmas. Alf Ventress circulated a description of the Traveller and its contents by radio, so within minutes, every patrolling constable was aware of the theft.

"What am I going to do if you don't find it?" she sobbed.

"Make sure she gets home, Constable," Sergeant Blaketon was firm. "And do something about that party. Then ask Greengrass what he knows about Mrs Hutchinson's car!"

"Claude wouldn't steal her car, Sergeant!" I protested.

"Ask him all the same!" and Sergeant Blaketon stalked out of the office leaving PC Ventress in charge of the hunt for Glenys' old car.

If you want news to travel quickly in Aidensfield, you make an announcement in the shop or you tell Edna. The village bush-telegraph then outsmarts any other system of news transmission, so within minutes of my return, I made sure everyone knew about the theft. Nonetheless, it was doubtful if we would trace the Traveller or its precious load. Our dilemma was whether to replace the stolen items now or wait in case the vehicle was quickly traced with its load intact. It was now 11am - the party was scheduled to start at 4pm for the children, with Father Christmas arriving at 6pm. We could tolerate a short wait but as I walked towards the hall while trying to determine a course of action, Claude Jeremiah Greengrass and Alfred, his scruffy dog, emerged from Claude's old truck outside the pub.

"Ah, Claude, I want a word with you," I hailed him.

"I know nowt about Glenys' car," were his first words.

"Not if it contained your Christmas present?" I put to him.

"My present?" he blinked. "What are you talking about?"

"You're a pensioner, Claude. You're entitled to a present."

"Pensioner? Me? You must be joking.."

"Your secret's out, Claude, we've a list from the Post Office."

He paused for a moment, then whispered, "Look, if this gets out, I'm finished. Who'll give me work if they think I'm too old and past it?"

"So, Claude," I smiled, "Let's make a deal - you tell me who's nicking those cars and I might forget you're a pensioner."

He blinked furiously then whispered, "I'm no copper's nark, you know, but, well, it's not decent, is it? Pinching presents for kids and pensioners."

"Very nobly spoken, Claude, so what can you tell me?"

He led me from prying eyes and told me that two Ashfordly youths were preying on cars left unattended during Christmas shopping expeditions. When the owners were out of sight, the lads would drive away the cars and steal any spirits, wines, beers or cigarettes before abandoning the vehicles.

"I'm not saying who it is, mind," Claude said, "I mean, I can't be seen grassing to the constabulary - but they drive them stolen cars into that old army camp in Speckledale. It's used as a scrap yard, you know, unofficial, like.." and he blinked repeatedly.

"Thanks, Claude."

"Is there a reward? Not that I want this making public, mind, but, well, a chap has to live..."

"Your secret will be your reward, Claude!" and I left him, realising that I now knew the source of his second-hand spares business. Within minutes I was on my way to collect Sergeant Blaketon and half an hour later, we drove deep into the moors to locate the deserted camp. There, among dozens of abandoned cars, ancient and modern, was the scruffy old Traveller. We had found a car thieves' dumping ground and Sergeant Blaketon was delighted.

"We'll mount observations on this place," he assured me. "I reckon we'll soon catch one of 'em red-handed!"

Glenys' Traveller still had the keys in the ignition but the spirits and Christmas fare had gone. The presents were intact however and so, having examined it for fingerprints, I drove it back to Aidensfield. I was fair to Claude - I removed his parcel so I could slip it to him beyond the gaze of the public and warn him to keep away from the old camp! We were able to obtain some more turkeys and spirits for the party and so, by the time everyone began to arrive, the drama was over.

Claude was wonderful as Father Christmas but the climax was Stanley Preston's presentation to Glenys. Everyone was delighted that Alec had come too; both he and Glenys were in their best clothes. This was unusual - had the couple discovered our plot? We felt not, we felt sure our surprise was complete. So why had Alec come? Perhaps the theft had unsettled Glenys and she needed his support? Was she blaming herself for what had happened? I began to wonder whether Glenys was going to give up her voluntary work. Clearly, she was going to announce something but before she did so, Stanley Preston mounted the stage. Glenys hurried forward.

"Before you say your thank yous," I heard her say, "I'd like to say something."

"There is a matter I must deal with first, Glenys," said Stanley firmly but very diplomatically. "And then you can take the stage - I'll do my thank yous afterwards."

He called for silence then began to praise Glenys for her selfless work. Standing before the crowd, she grew very embarrassed and then he said, "On behalf of the people of Aidensfield, Glenys, I would like to present you with this gift token. We wish you the happiest of Christmases... but we insist, Glenys, that this gift is personal, for you."

She was dumbfounded but Alec eased her onto the stage to collect it and she ascended the steps to loud applause. She saw the large amount on the token and began to weep with happiness, wiping her eyes with her free hand.

"This is so lovely," she sniffed. "And I know somebody who can use this..."

"No," Stanley interrupted. "It's for you, no-one else."

"It'll be for our baby," she said coyly. "At last, Alec and I are going to have a child. We can get some baby clothes and a cot...you've no idea how happy we are, we wanted you all to be the first to know. But it means I won't be able to organise the party next year..."

Her remaining words were lost among the joy which flowed towards Glenys, Alec and their unborn child as the snow gently descended upon Aidensfield that night.

CATH STAINCLIFFE

Cath Staincliffe is creator of the Sal Kilkenny mysteries, set in contemporary Manchester, featuring single-parent, private eye Sal Kilkenny who has to juggle the demands of work with those of parenthood. *Looking For Trouble* was short-listed for the Crime Writers Association's John Creasey Award (best first crime novel) and was serialised on Woman's Hour, BBC Radio 4. Two further Sal Kilkenny mysteries followed: *Go Not Gently* and *Dead Wrong*. Cath lives in Manchester with her partner and their three children.

Cath Staincliffe

WHO'S SMILING NOW?

I expect someone will be here soon. There was a blue light flashing a little while ago. I heard a bit of a commotion.

I couldn't be certain that it would happen tonight but I was ready. Fully prepared. He'd no idea what was coming. I'd no idea who he was. That didn't matter. He was all of them, any of them. He chose himself. I knew him when the time came.

I'd not got much sleep last night - too excited. Going over my plans. The hardest thing had been to work out which method to use. A gun was out - the very thought of it scared the life out of me. And I hadn't a clue how to get hold of one, even with all that talk about them being cheaper than trainers if you had the right contacts in Manchester. I don't move in those sort of circles. I wasn't strong enough to use my hands and I'd no martial arts skills. Just a woman. An ordinary woman. I thought about bricks and bats and pokers and the like but any of them would depend so much on how he was positioned when we found each other.

A knife seemed the best option. I'd a drawer full to choose from plus a whole set of sharp French cookery knives. Women often used knives. I knew that from murder cases in the papers, on the telly. Handy. There for the grabbing. Transformed from their role of preparing food to nourish and sustain life to that of taking it. Fitting, I reckon.

I followed my usual Saturday routine: shopping, housework, watering plants, tidying the garden. It's important to keep to a routine. That's what the doctor said. Especially now that there's just me. The tablets won't work magic by themselves, routine creates a sense of purpose. Stop it all unravelling again.

There was plenty of time after tea to make my final choice of weapon. I laid them all out on the kitchen table. The bread knife was long but more suited to sawing, the teeth might get caught, stuck on bone. I put that away along with the little vegetable knives that were too short and the shiny machete. The carving knife and the fish knife were left. The carving knife was longer, broader but not as easy to conceal. I chose the fish knife with its narrow curving blade, its acute point. Razor sharp. I'd filleted enough mackerel with it to know that. Mum swore by that knife.

I left the house at nine. It's only 500 yards to the parade of shops. I pop down there for cigarettes when I run out, for the paper or a video or a take-away. Getting wound up on the way, waiting for it to happen. Dreading it. Occasionally, I'd get off scot free, return home trembling with relief but mostly my fears were justified. And every time a little more anger got stuck on the big fist of it inside me. Like a tumour. Thursday night had broken all records. Four times. When I got back in I went wild with rage, smashed up the mirror for the noise of it. Every sliver like a little knife. Imagining my revenge. I'd had enough.

It was a clear, cool night. Autumn. Already dark. The earthy smell of rotting leaves in the air. Ahead I could see the light from the shops spilling onto the pavement.

I passed two of them waiting by the bus stop, my heart racing a little, but they weren't the ones. Two would have been very difficult. Another stood outside the off-licence. He looked at me sideways as I stepped up to the doorway. I felt my chest tighten. Try it, just try it. I looked back as I went inside, just a glance, my fingers curling round the knife handle in my coat pocket. He looked away.

I paid for my gin and cigarettes.

Perhaps simply carrying the knife was affecting things. Somehow they sensed it. Were more wary of exercising their power.

Turning back for home I spied another one waiting for the phone. A trickle of sweat tickled my armpit and slid down my ribs. My mouth was dry. I couldn't swallow. I was almost home. There was a young girl inside the booth. He stood by the garden hedge, smoking a cigarette.

I looked straight ahead, down a little, avoiding contact. Giving him a chance. I'd actually gone a step or two past him when he spoke.

I was surprised at how lightly I moved. I dropped my carrier bag, whirled round, knife in my hand. It slid through his jacket effortlessly, right up to the hilt. I didn't look at his face then, all my concentration was on the knife. At the edge of my vision I saw his arms coming up and forward towards me. I was still pushing on the knife. I leant forward, whispered. Quietly he toppled back over the low hedge and into the garden. He disappeared. So quiet. Like a dream. I could hear the girl in the phone booth laughing, her back to the pavement.

I picked up my carrier bag. The gin was all right.

It's been a good night for television. I've seen a lovely, old film. Black and white. *Looking After Baby*. Mum loved that film, knew half of it by heart. They don't write scripts like that anymore.

I'll miss that knife.

I'm not sure whether they'll understand if I explain it to them. It might be best to keep quiet. It's hard to think. The gin's made my head ache and I feel a bit queasy now. I explained it to him, so he'd know why. Only fair. As I was pushing, I leant close, whispered. I'm sure he could hear. I read somewhere that death sharpens all the senses and hearing is the last to go. So, I said it quietly but he heard me all right.

"Give us a smile." Echoing his last request. And he did. I looked then. Like a wolf, lips wide, teeth and gums exposed. Grinning. A real smile.

And I smiled back. A dazzler. One for him. For all of them. For all the times they'd asked for it.

"Give us a smile."

"It might never happen, give us a smile, love."

"Cheer up, darling. Give us a smile."

Give us a smile smile smile smile smile smile smile.

ALISON WHITE

Alison White was born and bred in Liverpool. She returned to the North-West after some time living and working in London and now lives in Southport. Her short stories have been published in many magazines at home and abroad and have also been broadcast on BBC Radio 4 and BBC World Service. A day job in Liverpool occupies much of her time, as does her family. When she escapes both, she writes.

Alison White

THE END OF THE PIER

Another wintry day. I used to see that as instant death to Southport, a seaside town. But not now. Even as the clouds thicken and darken over the sea, and the rain begins to come, things look good. Maybe to appreciate good you have to have tasted bad. And I can remember...

My phone was dead. I knew it was coming, red bills and warnings had made it clear, but I wanted the police, and fast. I'd have to walk round there, morning sickness or not. So I pulled on my coat, then head down with hands pushed deep into my pockets, faced the bitterness of the morning wind.

Southport's police station on Albert Road was only a five minute walk from my flat then, just off the promenade. But buffeted by the wind, and not feeling a hundred per cent, it took a bit longer. I had a copy of the local paper in my hand, hoping that when I got there, they'd tell me there was a mistake, and they'd printed the wrong picture.

I'd heard the reports on radio that a body had been found. On a stretch of land between the promenade and the new sea wall area, close to the now derelict mini-fair. Murder they said.

At the police station I unfolded the paper. "This picture," I said. "The dead man...is that definitely him?"

"It's a computer image," the officer explained. "And as good a likeness as we can get. Are you all right? You look very pale."

I shook my head. "I'm afraid I think I can help you."

'*DO YOU KNOW THIS MAN?*' the headline read. '. . . *thought to be a local man, a familiar figure in the town.*'

So familiar that no-one knew his name. Brutally assaulted and left for dead. No wallet, no papers. Just a familiar face that nobody had come looking for.

"His name," I told the police, "is Barney Bluster. He had a flat in town...I'm not sure where. Just that it would be right, from the end of the pier." I smiled faintly, remembering.

"Known him long have you?"

"We only met once," I explained. "Just a couple of weeks ago. But that's definitely him."

The police were lovely. They made me a cup of tea and let me tell them what I knew. Our only meeting, vivid in my mind.

I was just this side of despair when I first met Barney Bluster. Like him, I was sat early one evening, feeling sorry for myself in a steaming cafe. Its bright lights fighting valiantly against the fierce winter evening. The recent storms had wreaked flash floods and havoc in the town.

Usually it was lively to walk round. Away from Lord Street and the big shops, there were the little places. A jumble of coloured, plastic beach items and souvenirs. Novelties and gifts in the windows all year round. Pleasureland's cable cars, bobbing with the promise of summer fun. But now, some of the smaller shops stayed shuttered following the bad weather. As a rule, you could still walk halfway down the pier, but even that was closed off now while they checked it out after the storms. Not, I suppose, that many would choose to walk along it in this sort of weather. Only fools like me, who found it always fascinating. A jumble of iron, with the ghosts of summers past screeching on the wind, if you listened hard enough. If you cared.

I'd been drinking my coffee for about twenty minutes, making it last. Looking out of the window which periodically steamed up, at the bleakness outside. I wiped away some of the condensation with my sleeve. With a 'tsk' sound emanating from her lips, and aimed at me, the waitress bustled past. A vision in a multi-coloured nylon overall, she wiped the window herself, with a cloth specifically for that purpose.

Then I saw him. An elderly bloke, with rheumy eyes, the sponge-soaked nose of alcohol abuse and a dirty raincoat wasn't an obvious soulmate. We were both gloomy, yet saw the humour in the action of the waitress. For a second, our eyes flashed with shared laughter. Then we returned to our mugs and our private misery.

Still, I didn't expect to speak to him. Or even see him again. When I'd finished my coffee, I'd left the warmth and brightness of the muggy cafe and headed towards the promenade.

Even the seagulls screamed in protest at the bleakness of the day as they soared overhead. The promenade was decked with gazebos, Edwardian in style, their elegant ironwork immaculately painted. But dusty rain drizzled down the panes of glass, and the wind wrapped litter around the bench legs. Chip papers and crisp packets. I noticed some initials, freshly carved into the back of one of the benches with a brutality that didn't suit their declaration of love.

I'd always loved Southport. I was going to make it big, and have a huge place here to come home to whenever I wanted. Except it hadn't quite turned out like that. That's the trouble with being a woman. On the stage, your looks fade and die quicker than a summer flower, as someone once said. Those younger and more beautiful on their way up. And OK, more talented too. But I'd always got by.

But even though I'd been keeping up the payments on my debts, I knew this time I wouldn't finish the panto season. I'd been lucky to get this last run, which wasn't even in Southport but out in the wilds of Lancashire. At thirty-seven (but only admitting to twenty-eight) I was OK if you put me at the back and slapped on the scarlet lips - I could high kick with the best of them. But not when I was pregnant. So not for much longer.

Of course there were ways of sorting these things out. And I wouldn't have been the first dancing girl to have done that. But I couldn't. The father? Well - let's just say I reached out one night and that's about as much as I can remember. No, it's not something to be proud of but that would hardly be the child's fault would it?

So that night, I left the cafe wondering what to do with my life and whether it was actually worth going on with. Most nights, I'd have been twenty-odd miles away by then, shrugging into my tights, sweaty bodies clashing, in the cupboard they described as a 'dressing room.' No time to brood there. But it was my night off and I had time a-plenty to just wander around.

When the rain came again, I was by an amusement arcade. I went in, ignoring the teenager eyes glazed by the flashing lights and the electronic music, and made my way through the darkness to the tea bar at the back. That was when I saw him again. The old man from the first cafe. Like me, he was lost. We acknowledged each other with a nod. And it would have ended there if I'd looked where I was going. But somehow, I tripped, and ended up on my backside on the floor, polystyrene cup in the air, scalding tea snaking across the floor towards him.

"That's what I call making an entrance," he said, momentarily stirred from his lethargy.

I wiggled my legs to check for damage before I got up. Still had a few weeks kicking in me, didn't want to blow my last paychecks.

"I'll live," I pronounced, scrambling up. I'd given up on elegance long ago.

"Probably still play football," he murmured.

"Or dance." I turned to go and get another cup of tea but heard him catch his breath.

"Dance did you say? On the stage?"

"Mmm. Not the Southport Theatre though," I admitted, before he got excited. "Just a little place. A 'Village girl,' that's me. You know, chorus stuff in panto."

"Sit down." He indicated the chair opposite his. "I'll get you another drink. You rest your dancer's legs."

It wasn't a pick up. There was no flash of lewd interest in his eyes, just a flicker of interest in my life. And I grabbed at that. Who wouldn't? No-one else cared.

He shuffled back, this time with a large tea in a plastic mug and had even splashed out on a packet of biscuits. "For the shock," he explained, seeing my surprise. "Sugar is supposed to do something for it."

"Cheaper than booze I suppose," I said, snapping a biscuit in two. "You interested in the theatre then?"

He slurped his tea. His eyes, that once must have been almost turquoise, but were now yellow and bloodshot, focused somewhere off in the distance. "I was on the stage myself once. Barney Bluster. Comedian."

"Oh." I tried to look as though the name meant something to me, but he saw it didn't. "I know," he said sadly. "But once...well I was tipped to be a star. Even had a show on the pier. Not here, a little place in North Wales. But it was buzzing. Thirty years ago. Well before your time, you'd be just a girl then."

"Not now," I said.

"You're still dancing, that's something. You still get the calls."

"Not for much longer. I'm pregnant," I said. Glad to be able to tell someone. Even if it was some old bloke I didn't know from Adam, I'd probably never see again.

"That's not good then?"

"No."

"The father?"

"Forget it."

For a while he didn't speak, then sat back in his chair and stared into space again. Finally, "I envy you."

"My youth?" Which was laughable, but I presumed he was being comparative. It could be just about all he envied. About all there was.

"No," he said honestly. "The chances you still have. To make a difference. To make someone."

"It's easy to get that chance," I said. Even he could do that. But I kept that thought to myself, although he seemed to read it.

"Not so easy to see it through, though. Is that what you're agonising about?"

"I don't have the money to give me choices," I said. "That's my other problem. Debt."

"Ah."

That didn't look like an experience that had bypassed him. In fact, judging by the appearance of his clothes and his general unkempt air, I'd say he knew a damn sight more about it than me.

"I know about regret," he said slowly.

"Regret?"

"I told you, I was going to be a star."

"You had a pier show, that's a big star to some," I said, knowing it was true.

"Even dancers with shiny tights and spangles are stars to the kids who come to watch our show. You can see it in the little girls' faces."

"You're right," he said. "That's how it should be. Everyone involved in the stage is part of the magic. But I didn't see it like that. It was only worth it at the top. I was going all the way to the London Palladium."

"What happened when you got there?" I gave him the benefit of the doubt. Assuming that he did.

But his eyes told me he knew I was being kind.

"I had a few good runs here and there but kept my eyes shut to everything else. I kicked a lot of good stuff out of the way. My ego didn't want to be just a part of things, it was all or nothing. So I ended up nothing. And alone."

I shuffled in my seat. He might only be drinking coffee now, but the smell of spirit on his breath indicated another liking to me. Again, he read my mind.

"That came later," he said. "When I realised what I'd done. But you know what? That doesn't help either."

"So what is it you're telling me?"

"Stop worrying about what you want," he said, "And take notice of what you've got."

While I mutinously stared down at my drink, which didn't appeal now anyway, he shuffled off towards one of the fruit machines.

Why should I even listen to him? Drunken old has-been. Not even that, more of a never-was. And I was wasting my night off. I decided to go home and watch TV, while I could still afford the licence fee.

I'd seen the gang of teenage boys earlier on. Not always an uncommon sight in a holiday town. They'd cluster round fruit machines and arcades, interested only in their own activities, I hadn't given them a second thought. Now they'd gathered by a shuttered kiosk, and as I left, I saw one of them look at me and nudge another.

So what? I'd done nothing wrong, and if they intended grabbing my bag, well let them grab. My key was in my pocket and my bag would be no more use to them than it was to me. It was an empty decoration.

But as I passed, I saw how they were looking at me. And realised it wasn't my bag they were interested in.

"How much?" one said as I drew close. So that's what they'd mistaken me for.

I crossed the road, ignoring them and cut down one of the side streets. The wind was noisy, and I didn't hear the footsteps behind me. Only the voices as I took another short cut into a narrow back-road.

"How much? Go on?" There were two of them.

"Get lost," I said, trying to laugh it off, but my voice was shaky.

"Our money's as good as anyone else's. We saw you with that old bloke." The taller one sneered, and pulled at one of the friendship bracelets he wore on each wrist. Twirling the ends in his fingers, plaited threads of different colours. "Just me, then, love eh? You might even enjoy it."

If we'd been on the promenade, I wouldn't have been afraid, but here, it was deserted. No traffic, just the backs of houses and a few shops, with bin bags left out to be emptied, and bits of rubbish bouncing along in the wind.

"Scram," I said, knowing they sensed my fear.

"Oi!" Round the corner came a figure. "This way, quick!"

Barney Bluster, God bless him. He was shouting backwards, into the other road. "There's a bunch of lads got a woman cornered down here."

Whoever, if anyone, he was talking to, wasn't the issue as the lads swore and ran off calling me a few names as they did. I hurried towards Barney.

"Thanks," I said, unsteady on my feet now and seeing the scolding in his eyes. "I know," I agreed. "I should have known better. I was in a rush to get home."

He wiped his eye; suffering from the blast of cold night air, it had started to run. "It's not just you you're thinking about now. I'll walk you back."

So I linked my arm in his and we ambled along together. Some would say, even that was stupid, but I knew it wasn't. Just then, I'd needed an angel, and though on the surface an unlikely candidate, Barney Bluster had been just that.

"Tell me about the friendship bracelet on that lad," the police officer said. "And what he looked like. It might be important."

"I remember he wore them on both wrists." I closed my eyes then and gave as detailed a description as I could, remembering his distinctive jacket too. Then I asked why.

"We found one of those bracelets near the body. If we find this boy, he might be nothing to do with it of course. But everything helps."

I walked for a while before going home. Stopping to look at the pier. The night I'd walked back with Barney I'd asked where he lived.

"To the right as you come off the pier," he'd said, winking. "Having that pier show was my biggest thing ever. After that you measure everything from the pier. Any pier. It becomes a focal point." I knew what he meant.

On Southport's pier, you could still read the words, *'Seaward end of pier open 8 days a week Monday to Doomsday.'* Doomsday had certainly come for Barney Bluster.

I walked down to where they'd found him. Blue and white police tape still flew in the wind on the land by the long-closed minifair. A complete contrast to the summer-busy Pleasureland. Left for dead, a crooked man by a crooked house, with the end of the pier in sight. Once more, the seagulls screamed overhead. I knew how they felt.

I cried off the panto that night, not in the mood for swaying about on stage and carrying a flower basket. Like Barney had said, it wasn't just me I had to think about now. Maybe I should find another way for my show to go on.

A few days later, a boy was charged with Barney's murder. Later, the police thanked me. My description helped them find a boy wearing an identical bracelet to the one they found by the body. He also carried Barney's wallet and a key that fitted his front door apparently. Then he confessed.

"How did you find out where Barney lived?" I asked them.

"His landlord came forward when he saw the paper like you. Thanks to both of you, we've got the person responsible. Mind you, we don't know what he was thinking of going down there late at night. The lad followed him. Bluster should have known better."

I agreed of course. Nobody had run around the corner to save Barney.

I never went back into panto. Decided to find another way to make my life work. I lived in a place I loved, and thought maybe I could still find stardust somewhere, if I kept my eyes open. And I realised when you do, it's surprising what you can see. This time, staring into a cafe, rather than out of one, I saw a notice that 'help' was wanted. Within the hour I had a job, and the flat above that went with it. Suddenly my debts weren't so much of a problem.

"I'm having a baby," I told Diane, the owner, as she buttered bread for sandwiches.

"I've got kids," she said. "If you're honest and hard-working, so what? We'll work it out. I like the look of you."

So I got to wear a nylon overall and wipe up crumbs. And you know what? I found I enjoyed it. It beats high-kicking when your joints ache.

"It must be lovely, living here all year round," tourists say dreamily. "You're lucky."

I know they're right. It's something I've been working on these last couple of years.

Today, we open up our refurbished cafe, Diane and me. We've got on so well, we've gone into full partnership, now that I've finally got myself straight financially. Southport's on the up, there's a lot of money being ploughed into the place and the tourists are flocking.

Diane loved my ideas for a theatre-themed 'diner' type place. We've got lots of posters on the walls for the local theatres. Advertising the present, but not forgetting the past. Programmes, cast lists, photographs and props are all around the place. Me too, grinning out from a poster bill, as Cinderella, years ago. A glass slipper on a velvet cushion in a case near the counter. Even my name badge says 'Cinders.' I'm not planning to go into a song and dance routine at the tables, but you never know. I can definitely feel the magic here.

I was in a house clearance place looking for a few bits of cheap furniture, when I saw a dusty box full of memorabilia. One man's memories. One man's life.

'Top of the bill for the End of the Pier Show, it's Barney Bluster.' Then lots of autographed photos of Barney, in a checked sports jacket, grinning insanely, thirty years ago.

We've framed the biggest poster, and put it with an autographed photo, by a big silver star. All on the wall right at the back of the till. You can't miss it. There's another one of Barney on the door. I put it there this morning. The last one to go up, after I'd wiped the condensation off the windows. With a cloth and not my sleeve.

My son's excited now and pointing at the silver star. I scoop him up in my arms and carry him over to it, before I take him to Diane's. She's looking after him while I'm on work duty today. We've got it all sorted out just fine.

"Look Jake," I tell him, pointing at the photo up on the wall. "He's a very special man and we're never going to forget him. That's the famous Barney Bluster. He got to be a star."